SNARLY
AND  BEAST
THE

Also by Bryan Simpson

A Mission of Madness

A Very Dark Place: 12 Terrifying Tales

Love, Life and Death (Unfinished):
a collection of early poetry

Bronto's Big Adventure
(Illustrated by Sarah Simpson)

SNARLY
AND THE *BEAST*

BRYAN SIMPSON

WITH ILLUSTRATIONS
BY
NATALIE SIMPSON

BNR
PUBLISHING

ISBN: 979-8-9859140-1-6 (Paperback)
ISBN: 979-8-9859140-3-0 (eBook)

Any references to historical events, real people, or real places are used fictitiously. Names, characters, and places are products of the author's imagination.

Cover art and interior illustrations by Natalie Simpson

This book is dedicated, in loving memory, to my brother, Christopher Simpson.

We love you and miss you.

HOW IT ALL BEGAN

(PART ONE)

"No way!" Snarly screamed. "You do it!"

"Coward!" a woman in the crowd screamed back, spraying those unfortunate enough to be standing in front of her with spittle through clenched teeth. She was trembling and her face was red with anger—anger and fear, to be exact—just like everyone else in the crowd.

But Snarly looked on this sea of red with utter defiance. "You bet I am!" he agreed. He would not be made a fool of, not anymore. He would not play the part of the patsy. He would not be their errand boy. "I don't see anyone else volunteering! I don't see anyone else coming forth to slay the Beast!"

That did it. Now they were *really* mad. Everyone started shouting at him, all at once.

"How dare you!" and "Who do you think you are?"

"Someone must go!" and "You would have the Beast destroy us all?"

"Coward!"

"Coward!"

And more shouts of "Coward!"

Snarly thought for sure he was about to be stoned. Until, that is, someone cried out, "String him up!"

Deep down, he always knew this was how he was going to go out—death by angry mob. Everyone in the village hated him. He couldn't blame them, really; he wasn't the easiest to get along with. But this did seem a little extreme, even for them.

Fear can make people do crazy things, I suppose.

Snarly backed up, the incensed throng advancing upon him, inch by terrifying inch, until he felt the cold stone of a cold, stone wall. He watched as his neighbors closed in on him, their fists raised, their eyes bulging from their sockets.

He cowered down and waited for the pain to start, but then—

Wait.

Is this confusing? It just occurred to me that this might be a little confusing.

You see, I already know this story, and I especially like this part. It's scary, don't you think? Poor Snarly being forced to go and—well, we'll get to that. For now, I think I should back up, just a little. And, please, do let me know if I jump ahead of myself again—I have a tendency to want to skip to the really juicy bits.

Like most stories, though, it's probably best to start at the beginning. As for Snarly and the angry mob...

It All Started at Breakfast

(CHAPTER 1)

IT HAS BEEN SAID—ON MANY OCCASIONS AND BY PEOPLE who should know—that the world was once a very different place, compared to what it is today. In fact, everything was different, as you'll soon see. Unfortunately, there is very little evidence to support this, and so these stories are now regarded as myths and fairy tales rather than actual history.

You may be wondering, *How could something like that happen?*

Well, the main reason is that the different people, creatures, and beings of that time have all passed away, and, through the years, the rains have washed away their stories, earthquakes have swallowed up their homes and relics, and their descendants have abandoned imagination and magic in the pursuit of less noble aspirations.

Our story takes place in this long-ago land of magic and wonder, and it all begins with a strange, grumpy little man named Snarly Smallbottom.

Now, we've all heard stories of elves, dwarves, fairies, gnomes, and the like, but Snarly belonged to another race of beings that have long since been forgotten. They were known as the Manichers, because they resided along the banks of the Manich River, most of them settling in Sandwich Town. This is actually where we get our word *miniature* from (bet you didn't know *that*, did you?), as they were often said to be Manicher, or miniature, versions of men. And while it was true that they closely resembled the race of men, as a general rule, they were about one-and-a-half to three feet shorter.

On this fateful morning, Snarly the Manicher was in his miniature kitchen, scrambling up some not-so-miniature graybird eggs. (Graybird eggs were huge, by the way. They would be like ostrich eggs to you or me.) And he was really looking forward to eating them.

But, as he did most mornings, just as Snarly was scraping the last little bits of breakfast onto his plate, as if he had been waiting around the corner for that precise moment (and he probably was), Brutus jumped through the window and offered up his most pathetic "I'm hungry" meow.

"Oh, no you don't," Snarly said. "Not this morning. These are my last two eggs."

Brutus meowed again, overly exaggerated, as if he were starving to death.

"Well, I'm hungry, too. And I had to work for these, so go bother someone else."

Brutus tried a different approach and began to purr. And when that didn't work he brought out the big guns. He lovingly rubbed his head on Snarly's legs, weaving in and out, crisscrossing between them, in what he liked to think of as the fall-in-love-with-me-and-give-me-your-food-because-I'm-so-adorable dance.

But Snarly wasn't falling for that, either. He simply ignored the cat and walked over to his seat at the table, "accidentally" stepping on Brutus's tail along the way.

He laughed as the cat yowled in pain. "Serves you right, coming in here uninvited and begging for food," he said as he sat down.

Now it was Snarly's turn to take the lead. It was time for the ha-ha-I-can-stand-upright-and-have-opposable-thumbs-and-can-make-my-own-breakfast-on-a-hot-stove-and-don't-have-to-share-any-of-it-with-you dance.

A devilish grin on his lips, Snarly raised an eyebrow, keeping one spiteful eye on the hopeful Brutus as he slowly unfolded his napkin and carefully tucked it into his shirt collar. He licked his lips as he gently sprinkled just the right amount of salt and pepper onto his plate.

Brutus's tail twitched as Snarly picked up his fork and knife. After cutting a portion of the eggs, he held the fork up, turning it this way and that, examining it in the light.

Brutus didn't even blink. His eyes glistened as he watched the steam rising from the yellow and white sliver of heaven. His nose pulsed as he sniffed the deliciousness out of the air.

Oh, please, he thought. *Please, please, please, let me have just one small, tiny bite.*

But Snarly opened wide and put the fork up to his mouth.

He held the pose as he looked over at Brutus again, out of the corner of his eye, his grin gradually growing more and more devilisher.

Brutus gulped, and then Snarly finally—mockingly, heart-rippingly, dream-shatteringly!—put the big bite of eggs in his mouth. He closed his eyes as he chewed, clearly savoring it, then smiled a big, nasty smile at Brutus, egg sitting on his lower lip, and patted his belly.

"Now those are some good eggs," he gloated.

Brutus dropped his head with a quiet moan.

What you must understand is that Brutus was not Snarly's cat. Brutus was just a mangy stray that no one in the village liked, so it only made sense that the two should find each other.

Snarly often had scraps for Brutus, who was very thin and unhealthy-looking, and no one could understand why Snarly was so nice to the cat. (I mean, this was Snarly we were talking about!) But I guess everyone needs a pet.

In fact, it was Snarly who gave Brutus his name. When they first met, Brutus was in an alley beating up a dog over a discarded piece of meat. It was quite brutal to watch, and Snarly found it to be very amusing. He liked the unfriendly, grumpy cat. Lately, though, Brutus just seemed whiny and needy.

But still, he did look pathetic.

Snarly sighed. "Here," he said as he slid the plate over to the other side of the table. "I was wanting toast anyway."

Brutus hopped up onto the table and sniffed the plate. He eyed Snarly. Then, once he was sure it wasn't a trick, he began to purr—sincerely this time—and munch up the eggs.

Snarly scowled at the gray and white (and brown, from sleeping in the dirt) cat and headed back to the stove to heat his toast. That was when he heard the town bell begin to chime.

Now, the town bell was located in the middle of the village, and was only rung in emergencies (like when, during the Frost Wars, the village was unlucky enough to be in the path of an ice tornado) or times of extreme importance (like when the mayor's mother-in-law was visiting, and he tried to force the entire village to make him look good by saying nice things about him, like that he was so handsome and that he had wonderful, minty breath and that he was the best government official the land had ever known).

As far as Snarly knew, there were no important events planned. Maybe it was an emergency. Maybe they were all in some sort of danger.

He hurried over to the front window and started to open the curtain, to see what all the fuss was about, then caught himself and flung it shut again.

"What am I doing?" he asked Brutus. "Someone probably just got a papercut or something. Or misplaced their brain!" he laughed.

Brutus looked up and licked his lips, uninterested in whatever Snarly was talking about.

"Ah, who am I kidding. You have to *have* a brain to lose one."

But then he heard shouts as several people ran past his window. Whoever it was, they sounded scared. Snarly was curious, but he shook his head and turned away.

They're always making a big deal out of nothing, he thought.

With that, he was thinking about how, all his life, people have always complained about him. At one time, his parents even tried to get him to visit the medicine man/life insurance salesman who lived in the next village over, to hopefully cure him of his naughty nature.

But, alas, Snarly was destined to be the town grump.

He earned the name Snarly because, when he was born, he didn't cry like normal babies; it was more of a growl. And he always wore a frown. It would be true to say that Snarly was probably one of the worst babies in all the history of babies. He spit out his food, he whined, and he cried. And he would never go in his diapers. He would hold it, even as a newborn baby, and as soon as his mother or father would check to see if he had gone, right when their faces were up to his bum, that's when Snarly would let it rip.

Then, when he attended school, he took bullying to a whole new level. He would push girls into the mud and punch boys in the arm. No one was safe. But he didn't just bully the other kids. No, he would bully the teachers, too. Can you imagine, taking your *teacher's* lunch money?

That didn't last long, though, because Snarly graduated from school when he was only seven years old. Not because he was a genius, mind you, but because he was so bad. They just pushed him right through! His parents pushed him right out of the house, too, he was such a troublemaker. So, he got his own house and a job shoveling and bagging manure for fertilizer.

But he didn't get any better as an adult. In fact, some might say he got even worse. He cheated on his taxes, he never left a tip when eating at a restaurant, and one of his favorite things to do was to scare babies, on purpose, just to hear them cry!

Another frightened group of villagers ran past the house, returning Snarly's thoughts to the present. He thought he heard one of them shout something about the Beast.

Could it be? There hadn't been any word of the Beast in months.

He looked over at Brutus, who had finished the eggs and was now patiently waiting for his chance to beg for the toast.

He thoughtfully stroked his short, gray beard and frowned. Curiosity was beginning to push aside his better judgment. Snarly tried to avoid people as much as possible, seeing as how no good ever came from him going into town.

Just eat your breakfast and go to work, he told himself as he started to butter his toast. *Let them deal with their own problems.*

But, the Beast...

He sighed and dropped the butterknife on the counter. "I'm not going to get any peace, am I, Brutus? Might as well go and see what all the commotion is about." So, he grabbed his cloak and walking stick, tossing the toast on the table as he did so. (Brutus snatched it up right away.)

Outside, the sun shone brightly, and when Snarly squinted his eyes against it he looked grumpier than ever.

Once his eyes finally adjusted to the brightness, he gave a complaining growl and headed for the town square. And while this morning started out just like any other, it would soon prove to be quite the opposite, for today was the day that...(drumroll, please)...

The Final Knight Returns (sort of)
(CHAPTER 2)

HIS WHOLE LIFE, SNARLY HAD HEARD STORIES OF THE dreaded Beast. The Beast was a creature that terrorized the people of the land. If you believed the legends, it killed livestock, abducted children, and destroyed property, among other things. The problem was that no one had ever actually *seen* the Beast. They just knew of someone who knew someone who knew someone who had a cousin, or something, who had seen it. Kind of like Bigfoot.

There had always been a circle of twelve knights to protect the village, twelve brave men who had donned the armor and taken the oath, sworn to serve and protect all those who could not protect themselves. If a knight were ever to perish in battle, another brave soul would step up to take his place. It was a noble calling, to be sure, but lately, fewer and fewer had been brave enough to join their ranks. So few, that when one of the knights died, there were now none to replace him. One by one, they had volunteered to go out in search of the Beast, and, one by one, they had not returned.

The twelfth knight had been gone for three months, and no one had heard from him in all that time. And the people were getting restless. All of them, except for Snarly, that is. Snarly couldn't care less.

But something about today seemed different.

When he reached the town square, it looked as though everyone had shown up. The entire village was in an uproar. The last time Snarly could remember seeing everyone like that was at the Harvest Festival three years earlier, when a baby dragon had wandered onto the fairgrounds.

He tried to weasel and squirm his way to the center of the crowd, which was a very strange place for Snarly to be—in the midst, and all. He didn't usually get involved in such things. He preferred to stay to himself and mind his own business, but he was curious about what the knight would have to say. Plus, he was ready for this whole Beast mess to be over with, once and for all.

At first, Snarly couldn't tell if the crowd was cheering, jeering, or wailing. The people closest to him, the ones he could see, looked scared and confused, almost panicked.

Something bad must have happened, he thought. Then again, the people did tend to treat the knights a bit like celebrities. Maybe they were just starstruck.

Then Snarly started to make out some of what they were saying.

"What does it mean?" one man shouted.

"What are we going to do now?" asked another.

A woman holding a baby said, "Does this mean we have to leave?"

Snarly finally found the center of the mob. The mayor, Mayor Mortimer Mayer, was standing on a makeshift platform and holding a knight's helmet. Snarly looked around, but he didn't see the knight anywhere.

"Well, hello, Snarly!" It was his father, Festus. He was shouting, trying to be heard over the noise of the crowd. He looked very excited to be there—he was a bit of a gossipy Gus. (Gus was the town gossip, in case that wasn't clear.) "Surprised to see you here, Son."

"Hello, Father. Mother."

Snarly's mother, Brunhildia, went straight to fixing his unkempt hair. "My, my, Snarly, why won't you ever brush your hair?"

He tried to slap her hands away, but she was very insistent. "What's the point?" he said. "It's just going to get messed up again."

"Come to see what all the excitement's about?" his father asked, all smiles.

"Yes."

"I believe the mayor is trying to make an announcement on the situation now," said Brunhildia. "If everyone would just be quiet so he could talk."

The mayor had his hands held high in the air, trying to get everyone's attention. "People of Sandwich Town!" he shouted. "Please! Everyone, calm down! There is a note attached to the helmet! I'll read it, but I must have quiet!"

The people started to quiet down, but it took a while. It was like slowly turning down the volume on a television set.

When it was quiet enough, the mayor cleared his throat and read the note that was attached to the knightless helmet.

"The note reads as follows…"

After Mayor Mayer read the note, he looked back up at the crowd.

Everyone was silent, their eyes wide, their mouths hanging open in dreadful amazement. They were all beginning to see that the impossible was happening. The moment they had all feared, but never thought would actually come, was coming. They knew that they were now completely vulnerable to the Beast. No one would ever be safe again.

Then the roar of panic filled the air once more.

"What does that mean?!"

"It's all over!"

"We're doomed! Doomed, I tell you! DOOMED!!"

This time, the mayor just stood still and waited for the chaos to subside. When it finally did, he spoke calmly. "So, now we must figure out what to do next. Xavier was our last knight, the last brave warrior among us. We must defend ourselves now."

"How?!"

"We should fortify the village," he continued. "Build a wall. Make weapons. And while we do that, we shall send another hero to find the Beast, in hopes that he—or she— will be able to find and vanquish the threat before these provisions are needed."

There was a quiet murmur among the crowd.

"Now, who will be brave enough to take on this quest?" Mayer asked.

"Who else is there to send?" one man angrily shouted. "We are not soldiers! We are simple people! Farmers!"

"Yeah!"

"But someone *must* go," Mayor Mayer insisted. "Are there any suggestions?"

As everyone talked amongst themselves, Snarly began to notice that a lot of the people were glancing over at him. Their looks seemed to suggest that they were thinking something like, *We should send Snarly. Yes, Snarly, who we don't like. Snarly, who's always grumpy, has a bad attitude, who never smiles, and is always rude.*

Snarly didn't like where this was going. People had always looked at him like that, like they didn't want him around. It made him think of how the children of the village sang songs about him. There was one in particular he didn't like:

Snar - ly, Snar - ly, al - ways the grump.

Snar - ly, Snar - ly, fell on his rump.

It serves him right, it serves him well.

Oh, Snar-ly, Snar-ly, you sure do smell!

It wasn't the words that bothered him. For one, they were true, he did smell. For two, it wasn't a very well-written song. What bothered him was the annoying tune the kids put to it. It would get stuck in his head, and then the next thing he knew, he would be singing that very song, insulting himself!

Then someone said it. Someone deep in the crowd yelled, "I nominate Snarly Smallbottom!"

Boy, everyone loved that idea. They all started giving their approval.

"Wonderful idea!" Mayor Mayer exclaimed. "Snarly Smallbottom, you have been chosen for this great and mighty task!"

Snarly growled, "Oh, no you don't! No, no, no! You can't send me! I don't want to go!"

"But, you have been chosen," the mayor said, very matter-of-factly.

"So choose someone else!" Snarly snapped. "A hero would volunteer, and I don't volunteer! I'm no hero!"

"You must go!" a man in the crowd pleaded.

"I don't *have* to do anything!" Snarly said, defiantly. "Find some other fool!"

"Stop being so selfish!"

"Do it!"

Snarly screamed back, "No way! You do it!"

(If you'll remember, I believe this is where we started earlier.)

An angry, red-faced woman spit all over the backs of people's heads. "Coward!"

"You bet I am!" Snarly waved a finger over the heads of the unruly mob. "I don't see anyone else volunteering! I don't see anyone else coming forth to slay the Beast!"

And then everyone got really mad and started shouting, all at once.

"How dare you!" and "Who do you think you are?"

"Someone must go!" and "You would have the Beast destroy us all?"

"Coward!" "Coward!!" and "Coward!!!"

And just when they were about ready to hang Snarly, right there in the town square, a familiar voice rose above all the others. "Wait!" It was his father. "What are we doing? Look at us, we're all behaving like a—well, like an unruly mob. We must have order!"

The mayor finally took charge of the situation. He pushed his way to the center of the crowd and said, "Festus Smallbottom speaks the truth!" And then to Festus: "What do you suggest we do then, Festus?"

"Suggest?" Festus looked at the angry faces surrounding him, then at Snarly. He had no idea how to help his son out of this mess. "Uh, well…how about a vote?"

Mayor Mayer smiled broadly. "A village vote. Excellent idea!"

Now, one thing these people absolutely loved was voting. Raising a hand, shouting *Yea!* or *Nay!*, it was terribly fun. So, whenever someone suggested a village vote, the village voted.

The mayor stood tall. "Here now, all those in favor of sending Snarly Smallbottom in search of the Beast, signify your approval by raising your right hand and saying *yea*."

Immediately, everyone's hand (except Snarly's, of course, and, surprisingly, his parents') shot into the air, and with a thunderous roar, everyone shouted, "Yea!"

Snarly looked over the crowd and sighed. "Figures."

The mayor smiled a smug little smile at Snarly and said, "All those opposed?"

The only sounds in the village were the sounds of crickets and birds, with the occasional loud moo from a cow. Unfortunately for Snarly, their votes didn't count.

At this, Snarly snarled his deepest snarl, slowly raised his hand, and quietly grunted, "Nay."

He looked at his parents—who hadn't voted yes, but also hadn't voted no—hoping that they, at least, would side with him. Not that it really mattered at this point.

Mayor Mayer looked to Snarly's parents as well. He said, "Festus, Brunhildia, how do you vote?"

Not surprisingly, feeling the pressure of the crowd, his mother lowered her head, averting the gaze of her son, and his father said, "Um…undecided."

"What?!" Snarly shouted.

Festus shrugged. "Sorry, Son."

"Well, there you have it," the mayor said, cheerfully. "It is decided."

Snarly lowered his arm. "Great."

Usually, when one of the knights volunteered, there would be cheering and dancing, and they would carry the knight around on their shoulders. But for Snarly, there was nothing, nothing but more of those smug looks.

No, Snarly knew there was nothing left to do now but...

Pack a Bag and Say Good-Bye

(CHAPTER 3)

SNARLY LOOKED AT THE TATTERED, BROWN KNAPSACK and frowned. It was sitting on the bed, right in front of him. He had packed it many times before, to go on little camping trips, but he could not now think of what to do. What should he put in it? Did it even matter?

How do you pack for your death?

A grim thought, to be sure, but if the twelve knights were no match for the Beast, what could Snarly possibly hope to accomplish. Sure, he was a young man, only eighty-seven years old (That may seem old to you and me, but Snarly's race lived to be well over a hundred years.), but this was a task for a trained warrior.

Just then, Brutus jumped through the open front window, shattering Snarly's thoughts. Brutus was not a cat that always landed on his feet, and so he stumbled in and fell into a chair, tipping it over with a crash.

"Well, aren't you the clumsy one?" Snarly said.

Brutus hissed at him and jumped back through the window, snatching up a half-loaf of bread with his teeth on his way out.

"Hey!" Snarly gave chase, but when he swung the door open, Jobos, the village idiot, was standing there. He had his arm up, hand in a fist, ready to knock. When Snarly just stared at him, Jobos went ahead and knocked at the air.

"What?" Snarly said, irritated.

"Hi, Snarly. How are you?"

"What do you want?"

"Uh, maybe you don't remember me," the little man said. "My name is Jobos. I live—"

"I know who you are," Snarly said. "I just don't care. What do you want?"

"May I come in?"

Snarly growled and walked away, leaving the door halfway open. He didn't have time for this. He went back to the chest of drawers in his bedroom.

Jobos, who was a rather ugly, fat, buck-toothed fellow with horrible fashion sense, took this as an invitation to enter. "So, buddy," he said, "when do you leave?"

Buddy? Snarly thought. Who did this guy think he was?

"In the morning."

"Oh. Okay," Jobos said, and then just stood there, in the doorway, grinning stupidly and rocking on his heels.

Snarly, impatient as ever, said, "What is it that you want, Jumbo?"

Jobos held up a finger. "It's, uh, *Jobos*, actually."

Snarly just raised an eyebrow and looked down at Jobos' round belly.

"Ah. Yes. I see." Jobos laughed uneasily as Snarly put some clothes into his knapsack. "Classic Snarly. Anyways," he continued, "I was wondering, if it might be possible, if I could have your hourglass? Some clumsy cat jumped in my window last week and broke mine."

"And why would I give you *my* hourglass?" Snarly asked, offended. "Go make yourself another one. Or trade for it." He slammed the drawer closed.

Snarly's aggression was making Jobos a little nervous. "I don't mean right now. No, no. I was thinking, you know, after you leave, maybe I could have it?"

"When I leave?"

What is this idiot talking about? Snarly wondered as he shoved past Jobos and went into the kitchen.

"Yeah. You know...because you won't be needing it anymore..." Jobos waited for Snarly to show that he understood, but he clearly didn't, so he added, "After you're gone...?"

"Gone?" Then he scowled and shouted, "I'm not dead yet, you grave robber!"

"Not yet, no," Jobos said. He was trying to sound sympathetic. "But you are going after the Beast, aren't you?"

Snarly shoved an apple and some bread into his bag. "You know I am."

"Then, you're as *good* as dead, wouldn't you say?"

"You little twerp!"

Jobos held up his hands. "I don't mean any offense."

23

"Who's to say I won't prevail?"

"Well, everyone."

He had a point there. "I suppose."

Jobos cheered up a little. "So, I can have your hour-glass?"

Snarly sighed and roughly tightened the straps on the knapsack. "Sure," he said. "Whatever. Who cares."

"Thanks, buddy!" And then Jobos, the village idiot, jumped up and ran out of the little house with Snarly's hour-glass.

"Hey!" Snarly ran after him but stopped in the doorway. "You said *after* I left!"

But Jobos was already gone. "Woo-hoo!" he hollered. "Hey, everyone, if you want dibs on Snarly's stuff, you better get in there!"

Snarly slammed the door. *Great,* he thought. He could just picture it now, all the freeloaders, those little scavengers. His house was going to look like the market on Squirrel-on-a-Stick Day.

Outside, Jobos ran past Snarly's father. "Hello there, young Jobos," Festus said with a wave. "Fine day, isn't it?"

"Yes, sir, it certainly is!" Jobos said as he waved back, not really watching where he was going. "You better get in there and pick out what you want before everyone else shows up!" And then off he went, skipping on down the road, happy and goofy as always. Skip, skip, skip, laughing and singing…until he tripped and landed flat on his fat face, the hourglass flying out of his hand and shattering.

"Oh, man."

What an idiot.

A little while later, there was a knock at the door. Snarly opened it to find his parents standing on his porch.

"Hello, Son. How are you?" asked his father. He had a big smile on his face.

"How do you think I am?"

"Oh, come now, Snarly," his mother said as she pushed her way into the house. "Don't be like that."

Snarly shut the door behind them. "How should I be?" he said. "I have to go find this stupid Beast and try to kill it. And we all know how that's gonna end!"

"Hmm. Not very well, I assume."

"Festus!"

"Well, he's right," said Snarly. "This is a suicide mission. That Beast is going to rip me apart and make sandwich meat out of me!"

"Not necessarily," said Brunhildia.

"And why do we keep sending one knight at a time, anyway? Why not send an army?"

Festus shrugged. "That's just the way it's always been done."

"It doesn't make any sense!"

Snarly waited for more of a response, maybe some words of wisdom, but Festus just stared at him and then shrugged again.

Frustrated, Snarly put a hand to his forehead.

Brunhildia patted his back. "You've got to think positive, Son."

"Yeah. Positivity. That'll show the Beast."

Festus was looking around. "So, is it true, Snarly? What I heard?"

There was a long pause as Snarly waited for his father to finish, but, apparently, that was it.

"Is what true? How would I know what you've heard? I don't have your ears."

"Well, everyone's talking about it."

"Talking about what?" Snarly was getting tired of this conversation.

"That you're giving all your stuff away."

"No," Snarly said, "that is not true." Then, "Wait. Is that why you're here?"

"No, no, no," said Brunhildia. "Of course not. We just wanted to see how you were doing, that's all. Make sure you weren't too nervous."

"Although…"

"Festus."

"Brunhildia."

"Don't."

"I was just going to ask—"

"Now's not the time."

"Just ask already!" yelled Snarly.

Festus smiled. "Do you think I could *borrow* your shovel while you're gone?"

"You mean, can you have it? After I leave? To go get eaten by the Beast?"

"No—"

"I can't believe you guys!"

"Hey," said Festus, "we stopped an angry mob from hanging you. What more do you want?"

Snarly threw his arms into the air. "Oh, well, thank you *sooo* much!" he said, mockingly. "You could have voted *with* me, you know?"

"And have them turn on us? No sense in us all getting killed—uh—you know—killed with their rudeness, is what I mean."

"I know what you mean!" Snarly snapped. "Just take your shovel. You can use it to dig my grave! After the Beast kills me!" He plopped down into his chair next to the fireplace.

"Well, actually, that's Gorky the gravedigger's job—"

"Festus!"

"Plus, if it eats you, there probably won't be anything left to bur—"

Brunhildia slapped Festus upside the head.

"Hey!"

"Don't you know when to be quiet?" she scolded. "Go get your shovel, you big oaf!"

Festus held up his hands. "All right, all right," he said. "Sorry, Snarly. I didn't mean anything by it, you know that."

Snarly didn't even look up, just kept staring into the empty fireplace. "Mm-hmm."

Once Festus was through the back door, off to get his new shovel, Brunhildia turned to Snarly. "Don't worry, dear. Everything will be fine. You'll go out there and slay that ugly Beast, and then you'll come back home a hero. You'll see."

"Sure. Thanks."

"You're welcome, sweetheart."

Snarly gently rocked back and forth in the chair as his mother stood there, a little awkwardly.

You gotta give her credit, she almost made it, almost resisted the temptation. But, in the end, she just couldn't help herself.

"Snarly?" she asked.

"Yeah?"

"You don't, by any chance, still have that large casserole dish I let you borrow, do you?"

"Mother!"

"What? I don't want anyone to take it, that's all. It belonged to my great-grandmother, you know."

Snarly grumpily got out of the chair and huffed his way into the kitchen, mumbling to himself the whole way. "I'll get you your precious casserole dish," he said. "I'm gonna die and all anybody cares about is taking my stuff. Bunch of greedy, selfish—I oughta break it is what I oughta do..."

And that's how it was all day long. Snarly waited for someone to come along, someone to be a friend to him. But no one else came, except to pilfer through and tag his belongings, just in case. It was almost as if they all hoped he *wouldn't* make it back.

Who was he kidding? Of course that's what they were thinking. He was grumpy, mean, sarcastic, and, well, snarly.

Who would ever want to be friends with a jerk like me? he thought. *After it eats me, the Beast will be the hero! And they'll probably throw an annual feast to celebrate the day they finally got rid of me!*

He pictured all the villagers, bringing gifts to their guest of honor, the Beast, while bashing ugly little Snarly-piñatas. There would then be a parade that glorified the Beast, and it would end at the cemetery, where everyone would wait in line for their turn to spit on his grave. And there would no longer be stories of the Beast to frighten the children. No, they'd tell stories to bad kids about Snarly. "You don't want to end up like him!" they'll say.

But still, Snarly waited (because, secretly, he didn't want it to be true). In fact, he stayed up and waited all night, all the way to...

Midnight

(CHAPTER 4)

HE'D MADE A FIRE. SOMETHING ABOUT BEING ALL ALONE and lonely made a house feel colder and darker than it probably actually was. As he sat there in front of the fireplace, watching the fire dance and pop, Snarly heard the bells toll for midnight. He closed his eyes and slowly dropped his head.

The day was over. No one had come by to wish him luck or to say that he would be missed.

Sure, those wanting his stuff offered fake smiles and phony words of encouragement, but that was all. His own parents didn't even seem all that upset.

Snarly's familiar frown turned into something else then, a different kind of frown. It wasn't the usual grumpiness. He was feeling a sadness he had never known before. (Being all alone and lonely had also made the walls he had put up, to keep others out, feel more like a prison, bearing down on him and *keeping* him all alone and lonely.)

He wished Brutus was there. He should have petted the cat, just one more time, but he hadn't come back.

Maybe at breakfast.

Snarly looked back into the fire and sighed. *Today is the day I die,* he thought.

And then he went to bed, where he tossed and turned for several hours before finally falling asleep.

"Be sure, my friend, you will not die on this day."

Snarly snapped awake and looked across the room to find Brutus sitting on a rug and wagging his tail. Looking down, he saw that he was back in his chair, sitting next to a crackling fire.

How strange. Had he fallen asleep in the chair and dreamed of going to his bed?

His eyes moved around the room, but he saw no one, save the scruffy little cat.

Then, whose voice had he heard? Had that been a dream as well?

Doubtful—and feeling a little foolish—Snarly leaned forward in the chair and asked, "Brutus?"

Brutus bowed his head slightly. "Yes," he said. "Hello, Snarly."

"You can talk?" Snarly said in amazement. "No way. I must be dreaming."

"Of course you're dreaming. I'm a cat. Cats can't talk."

"Right."

Then Brutus stood, stretched, and walked toward the front door. "Follow me," he said as he began to float in the air.

Snarly watched as Brutus moved *through* the door, like a ghost. *Incredible!* He jumped up and crossed the room in a hurry, not wanting to lose him. He grabbed the doorknob and pulled, but the door wouldn't open.

He stepped back.

It's a dream, he thought. *Things work differently in dreams.* He understood then that he had to walk through the door, too, just like Brutus had done. So, he closed his eyes and stepped forward and—*SMACK!*—door right in the face.

Brutus poked his head through the wood. "What are you doing?"

"The door wouldn't open," Snarly said. "I assumed I had to go through it, like you did."

"Just unlock it, doofus."

Snarly reached up and unlocked the door. "Oh."

"Now come on, we've got a lot of ground to cover."

Once Snarly stepped outside, he was whisked away, up into the air. "Whoa!" he shouted as he tried to get his balance. He wasn't the biggest fan of heights—in fact, he was terrified of them—so he wasn't exactly thrilled about being so high up that he could see the rooftops of the entire village. He stared down, wide-eyed, and just kept repeating, "...please wake up, please wake up, please wake up..."

"Look, Snarly." Brutus put a paw on each side of Snarly's face to help him focus. "You must pay attention now." When Snarly tried to look down again, Brutus shook him a little. "You won't fall." And then, a little more gently, "I will keep you safe. I promise."

Though uncertain, Snarly nodded.

"Good," said Brutus. He pointed, beyond the village, over the horizon. "Your journey is a simple one, yet very dangerous. Come now, and I will show you the way."

And off they went, flying forward, as if gliding on a current of air. Brutus was very graceful—much like what you would expect a cat to be—but Snarly had a difficult time. It felt like he was being pulled along speedily, and he was continually trying to catch up with the movement.

"You must begin by entering the Whispering Woods," instructed Brutus. The two soared high above the trees as Brutus mapped out the way. He looked back, a slight grin lighting his feline face. "This will be the easy part." Then he got serious again and pressed forward. "From there, you will travel through the Black Forest."

Snarly watched as the ground moved below them. He saw a bridge, which crossed a narrow stream, separating the two woods. The night air was cold against his face, drying out his eyes. He tried to blink moisture back into them. He had to see what Brutus was showing him. He had to remember as much of this dream as he could.

"But you must be very careful," Brutus continued. "Try not to draw too much attention to yourself."

"Why?"

"Because, my friend, you won't want anyone to know you're coming. Once you breach the barrier into the Pretty Forest—"

Snarly's eyes went wide. "The Pretty Forest? Are you crazy? I'm not going in there!"

"You must," said Brutus. "For it is there, in the center of that dreadful place, that you will find the Beast's lair."

"The Pretty Forest," Snarly said in disbelief. "How could I possibly survive such a place?"

Snarly looked down and saw a great wall of plants. And then the darkness that was Pretty Forest—such a despicable place, it causes me discomfort to even write about it. But I must, in order to tell this story. Just keep in mind, if you happen to find yourself a little unnerved, that this ancient woodland no longer exists, so all of us reading about it today are perfectly safe. ;)

And then, quite suddenly, Brutus stopped.

Snarly came to a clumsy, skidding standstill beside him. His arms were flailing about, and he was leaning forward, as if teetering on an unseen ledge. Brutus put a paw on his shoulder, and he steadied out.

"Fear not, Snarly, I will be with you on your journey, as will others."

Snarly lowered his eyes to the small clearing below. He could barely make out what looked like a cave. He gasped. "The Beast?"

But instead of an answer, the ground began to rush past them, retracing the way they had come, but in reverse. "You must remember the path I have shown you, Snarly. That path will be your only hope of survival."

And then the scene below came to a dead halt.

"But what if I forget—"

"Good luck," said Brutus, and then he tapped a paw on Snarly's forehead.

Snarly instantly lost his balance again and began to sink back down toward the earth. He stretched out his arms, reaching to Brutus for help. "Hey! I'm falling!"

"It's time to wake up now, my friend," Brutus said with a smile. "Just remember what I said. Remember what I've shown you."

Snarly started falling faster and faster, and right before he hit the ground, he shielded his eyes—

—and woke up with a start.

He was sweating, and his breathing was heavy. He started to calm down once he realized he was safe in his own bed, but then jumped into a seated position when he felt something move near his feet.

It was Brutus, his tail swaying happily from side to side. "Brutus?"

That familiar, hungry meow.

Snarly relaxed a little. He must have overslept—that was the only time Brutus gave wake-up calls. But still…

"You came to me in my dream," Snarly said, eyeing Brutus suspiciously. "You spoke."

Brutus just stared back at him.

"Say something now."

But Brutus only meowed again, a little more urgently. He needed breakfast.

"I knew it. Just a dumb dream," Snarly said and rolled over.

Outside, the birds were chirping and the sun was shining. He wished he didn't have to get out of bed. He didn't want to admit it, but he was scared. He knew he had no choice, though. If he refused again, the villagers would hang him for sure, and no vote would be able to save him.

Brutus nudged him with his paw.

Snarly grumbled and threw back the covers. He got up and put on his robe and went to prepare what he assumed would be his last meal.

"Come on, you dumb cat," he said. "Let's get you some toast."

In the shadows, under the chest of drawers, a pair of dark, beady eyes watched as Brutus hopped off the bed and followed Snarly into the kitchen. Once the owner of those eyes was confident that no one would see him (or her, I'm not giving you any clues yet!), then he/she scurried away.

He/She/It didn't want to miss the...

Farewell Parade

(CHAPTER 5)

SNARLY PUT THE LAST OF HIS SUPPLIES IN THE KNAPSACK, buckled it up, and took one last look around his home (because he honestly didn't think he'd ever return). He then strapped on his sheath and inserted his short sword. Not much of a weapon against a monstrous Beast, but it was all he had.

Begrudgingly, he threw on his cloak and snatched up his walking stick, but then paused at the door.

"You really did it this time, you know that?" he said to himself. "Dummy."

He stood there a moment longer but knew there was no sense in trying to stall any further, so he took a deep breath and opened the door.

The first thing Snarly saw when he stepped out onto his porch was a couple of people standing on the other side of the road, arms folded, faces all scrunched up in a scowl.

He had a feeling that might happen, that certain of his fellow citizens would be waiting outside, just to make sure he carried out his *un*optional, *un*voluntary, *forced*-upon "responsibility." If he would have been any later in taking off they probably would have started pounding on his door.

Just ignore them, he told himself.

He walked down the narrow walkway to the front gate, slowly swung it open, and stepped out onto the road.

He looked back at the little house. True, it wasn't much to look at—he hadn't really bothered keeping up with the place. It didn't have fresh paint or any flowers in the windows. The yard was mostly weeds, overgrown. There was a garden, but it consisted of radishes and onions and the like. And more weeds. But it was his and he liked it.

He was going to miss it.

As he walked down the dirt road, the people of the village stood outside and watched him go. Normally, they would be standing on either side, lining the road, all the way down, everyone cheering and clapping. They'd be waving flags and jumping up and down, full of pride and optimism. But for Snarly, it was less like a parade and more like a funeral procession. No one cheered. No one said good-bye. No one waved or told him good luck. They just stood back, in their own yards, glaring at him.

Well, good riddance, thought Snarly. *Who needs you!*

He was feeling very discouraged—and scared and angry and nauseous—when a little girl with a pale blue ribbon in her hair ran up to him and held up a flower. It was a beautiful flower, but he didn't understand at first. What did she want from him? What was she trying to pull?

A lot of thoughts ran through his mind, out of habit. Thoughts like, *Bug off!*, *Scat!*, *Scram!*, *Get lost!*, and *Leave me alone!* But then he understood. She was giving it to him.

And so, since this was the only person who seemed to care, he took the flower.

"What is this for?" he asked.

The little girl sheepishly responded, "For luck," and then ran off.

Her mother snapped her fingers and pointed to a spot next to her. "Jasmine, get over here!"

Snarly watched her run away. "Thank you," he said, quietly.

For a moment, he wished all the children of the village weren't so afraid of him. Maybe he should have been nicer, less intimidating.

He shook away the thought. He had a long journey ahead, and he couldn't stop or let regrets slow him down now, so he continued walking, through this gauntlet of shame, with his head hung low.

As he neared the edge of town, Snarly noticed that someone was blocking the road up ahead. It was his parents, standing there with the mayor. *What now?* he thought.

When he got to them, he stopped, and they all just kind of looked at each other for a minute.

Finally, Festus nudged Mayor Mayer, who then cleared his throat and said, "Right. Gather around, everyone! Gather around!" And when they did he continued.

"Whenever one of our brave knights would set off on his journey to find and slay the Beast, we would have a parade and bid him farewell. It is only right that we do the same for Snarly...even though he didn't volunteer and is only going now because he has no choice. But anyways... Snarly, we wish you good luck on your quest."

There was a very weak applause from the crowd.

"Gee, thanks," said Snarly.

"Good luck out there, Son," said Festus as he shook Snarly's hand.

"My brave little man!" sobbed Brunhildia as she covered his face in wet kisses.

"Okay," Snarly said as he tried to push her away. "Okay. Okay, that's enough!"

"Sorry."

"Your mother's just excited," said Festus. "You know how she gets. She hardly slept a wink last night. Worries too much, is what I always tell her."

"He does tell me that," Brunhildia said, and then burst into tears again.

After Snarly finished drying all the spit off his face, he said, "Well, Father, how would you like to come along with me? We could have us a little father-and-son, Beast-slaying adventure."

"Oh, uh, well, you know," Festus stammered, "I would, you know that, but I've got that pesky back problem." He put a hand on his lower back and winced.

"You mean that back problem that only seems to flare up when you're asked to do something, like chores or risk your life helping your son?"

40

"That's the one. And wouldn't you know it, that blasted thing started acting up again just this morning."

"Yeah. I get it."

"I don't want to rush things," said the mayor, "but you should probably get going, Snarly. Don't want to keep the Beast waiting!"

"No wise words of encouragement for the boy, Mayor?" asked Festus.

"Well, I suppose…uh…*try* not to get yourself killed?"

At that, the crowd erupted in laughter.

"Wow," said Snarly. "Thank you for your support. And the boost of confidence."

"Don't listen to them, Snarly," said Brunhildia. "I know you'll know what to do when the time comes."

"I'm sure I will, Mother."

"Here," she said, and handed him something wrapped in a napkin. "I made you a teensy crinkleberry pie. I know it's your favorite."

Snarly smiled and hugged his mother. He was grateful for, and a little surprised by, the gesture. "Thanks."

He turned to the crowd. This was usually the point where the brave knight would make his heroic speech, filling the villagers with a certain certainty, making them feel all warm and fuzzy and safe inside.

Snarly opened his mouth, willing to comply with the formality—if only for formality's sake—but then he saw the looks of disgust on their faces. They hated him. They didn't believe in him. Why should he do any more for them than what he was already doing? He was already giving his life. What more did they want?

So, instead of saying anything, he just grumbled at them and waved a dismissive hand.

You don't deserve a speech, he thought.

He started walking, and there was one short-lived moment of hopefulness when he thought he saw Brutus, out of the corner of his eye. Maybe he'd want to tag along. He wouldn't be much help against the Beast, but he could provide some company, make the trek a little less lonesome.

But, alas, it was a different cat, an eerie black thing that Snarly didn't recognize. It just sat there, intently watching him, through golden brown eyes, and flicking its tail into the dirt. Just another looky-loo.

Even the animals in this village hate me, Snarly thought as he officially crossed the town line and headed off...

IN SEARCH OF THE BEAST

(PART TWO)

HOW WE DOING SO FAR? GOT A LITTLE GLOOMY THERE FOR a second, didn't it?

Yeah, I'm sorry about that, but I had to show you what life was like for Snarly. Character growth and all, you know?

Don't worry, though, things are going to brighten up for our little friend…then they'll get dark and grim again, then it'll get better, then sad, then…well, you know how stories are.

I'll try not to interrupt again. I just wanted to check in with you and make sure you were still with me. I mean, what's the point of telling a story if no one's around to read it, right?

Not that I think you're the type that would start a book and not finish it. No, no, no. I can tell you're a very dedicated and intelligent person, one with impeccable taste, who knows a good book when they see one.

Anyway, we should probably get back now, as Snarly is already well into…

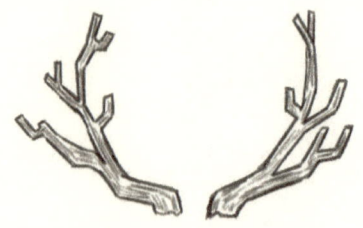

The Whispering Woods
(CHAPTER 6)

SNARLY STARTED HIS JOURNEY TRYING TO REMEMBER THE path that Dream-Brutus had shown him. The talking cat had told him it was his only chance of survival, of success. After a while, though, he shook his head.

"Superstitious mumbo jumbo…"

But, somewhere in that mind of his, he must have believed that the dream was more than just a mere dream, because he kept walking that same path.

For the moment, Snarly actually felt pretty calm. He liked it in the small, wooded area near his village. He had to go there often, in search of food and firewood. He found the woods to be very peaceful. He enjoyed the sounds of small animals scurrying about, birds chirping and singing to each other, and the smell of leaves and dirt.

He'd had the thought once before that maybe he should leave Sandwich Town someday and build himself a little cabin out there in the woods.

Maybe I should abandon this foolish quest and start building that little cabin right here and now, he thought.

No. He couldn't do that. If anyone found out, they'd probably come out here and hunt him down. Better to just finish the task.

Or, more accurately, let the task finish him.

Snarly shook his head again. He had to stop thinking that way; it wasn't doing him any good. But he knew what the problem was: it was that stupid, giant forest that was troubling him. Pretty Forest. That looming, impending threat hanging over his head. He just couldn't fathom how he might survive it.

But he had to push that horrid place out of his mind for now. Besides, the Black Forest would need his attention before he ever got that far.

When he was little, he had gotten lost in the Black Forest. His mother and father had told him many times to never go there alone, but he'd ran away from home, so he hadn't really cared what they had to say at the time. Whispering Woods had a lot of trees, but there were also a lot of landmarks and paths to help you find your way. Black Forest, on the other hand, was huge, and the trees were so dense that you couldn't see very far ahead, making it hard to know if danger was near. It was very easy to get lost, even as a skilled adult. After getting lost the one time, Snarly had never gone back. In fact, he was now farther than he'd ever been since that day.

He tried to set those nagging, fearful thoughts aside and just enjoy this part of the journey, while he still could. He was in the area of the woods that gave it its name. Here, the trees were denser, but the kind of trees that populated the area made it lighter instead of darker.

Snarly looked up in awe. He'd forgotten how beautiful it was there (the older he got, the less time he took to think about such things). When he'd run away, he was only three years old, and he was standing the same way now that he had then.

His eyes glistened in the fluorescence of the whispering glow trees. These trees took in sunlight from above and transferred it underneath. They also had reed-like branches, open on the end, so that when a breeze blew over them, it was as a thousand voices, whispering.

He decided this would be a nice place to stop and eat lunch before, you know, getting to the really bad part. As he ate his lunch under the trees—some cheese and bread, with the teensy crinkleberry pie for dessert—he listened to their calming whispers and basked in their warm glow.

Not long after he finished eating, while leaning against a tree and relaxing, smelling the flower the little girl had given him, Snarly heard the snap of a twig close by. He quickly grabbed his small knife, the one he had used to cut the cheese (ha ha) and jumped up, standing alert. He could hear someone, or something, moving around out there; he just couldn't see anything. But he knew it was getting closer.

"Who's there?" he shouted, his voice a little shaky.

After a moment, a large timber deer stepped forward from amongst the trees.

Snarly hadn't even seen it at first, not until it moved, because the coat of a timber deer resembled so perfectly the bark of a tree, giving it amazing camouflaging abilities against predators. Strengthening this illusion was a huge rack of antlers that looked like branches. And it wasn't afraid of Snarly at all. In fact, it walked right past him to the other side of the clearing. Snarly watched it, impressed by its size (and just a little nervous).

Before the deer disappeared back into the woods, it turned around and looked at Snarly again. It stamped its hoof into the dirt and whipped its head toward the trees.

Snarly frowned at the strange behavior.

The deer exhaled loudly and whipped its head toward the trees again.

Was this thing wanting him to follow it?

And then, as if in answer to his question, the timber deer did it a third time, stomping twice.

Then it walked on, into the woods.

Weird, thought Snarly. But he was done with his lunch, so he took the supposed advice from the deer and went on his way.

The rest of the trip through Whispering Woods was uneventful, but Snarly knew that the Black Forest was just around the corner. And he was not looking forward to it. In fact, it was *so* close, that in the same moment he thought those thoughts, he moved aside some brush and found himself looking at the stream that separated Whispering Woods from the Black Forest—the same stream he had seen in his dream.

Wonderful, he thought.

But he could see the Black Forest on the other side, and it didn't seem all that scary. Yet. So, he took a deep breath and stepped onto the narrow bridge.

Right away, a grainy, gargly voice said, "Who goes there?"

Snarly nearly jumped out of his boots, he was so startled. He looked all around, but he didn't see anyone. Because there was no one to be seen. The voice had come from under the bridge. "Who's there?" he asked.

"I asked you first," replied the voice.

Snarly puffed out his chest. He wasn't about to be intimidated by some bodyless voice coming out from under some stinky bridge. "I am Snarles Smallbottom!" he exclaimed. "Now who, and where, are you?"

"I am Boggwyn, the troll that guards this bridge."

"You guys actually do that?" asked Snarly.

"I do."

Snarly could hear movement under the bridge—lots of shuffling around, what sounded like dishes, or something, falling over—but, so far, no one had appeared. "Well, come on out from under there, then," he said. "Let's get this over with."

"Get what over with?" asked Boggwyn as he climbed out from under the bridge.

"Don't I have to pay a toll or answer a riddle, or something?"

Boggwyn looked confused. "No. I just make sure no one vandalizes it."

Now, Boggwyn looked friendly enough—some trolls were extremely mean and dangerous—but, man, was he ugly. He had greenish-brown skin, a huge, flat nose, big ears that had floppy tips and droopy lobes. The patch of hair on top of his lumpy head looked as though it hadn't been washed or combed in years. He wore tattered, dirty clothes. And he dragged around a huge club, which was just a common staple among trolls everywhere. And though he was fat, he wasn't very big. He was only a little bit taller than Snarly.

"Say," Snarly said, "aren't you kind of small for a troll?"

Boggwyn looked offended. "Trolls come in all sizes. I'm a dwarf troll. That's why I've been assigned to guard this smaller bridge. Well, that, and my brothers always make me pick last."

"Yes, well, anyway—"

"Hey! Wait a minute!" Boggwyn put a hand to his mouth and gasped. "You're not planning on going into the Black Forest, are you?"

"Well, yeah. That is where this bridge leads, is it not?"

"It does, but—you know it's scary in there, don't you?"

"Of course I know the Black Forest is scary. Everyone knows that."

"Then why would you go in there?"

"I won't be there long. I'm just passing through."

"Oh. Good." Boggwyn looked a little relieved. "Well, where *are* you going?"

"I must go to the heart of the Pretty Forest."

Boggwyn gasped again. "You don't want to go there," he said as he slowly shook his head.

"I must," said Snarly. "I am in search of the dreaded Beast."

Boggwyn gasped again, this time extra loud and extra long. "The Beast?" he asked in amazement. "Oh, not the dreaded Beast." Boggwyn cowered and cringed at the very mere mention of the Beast…and then realized he had no idea what the little man was talking about.

"What's the Beast?"

Snarly couldn't believe his ears. "'What's the Beast?'"

"I don't know," said Boggwyn.

"You mean to tell me you've never heard of the loath-some, odious, murderous, despicable Beast? That foul creature that terrorizes these lands, killing and maiming simply for its own sick pleasure?"

Boggwyn's eyes got really wide. "No. And I don't think I should like to hear about it now, either," he said and stuck his fingers in his ears.

"That's not too surprising, I suppose," Snarly said, more to himself than to Boggwyn. "The Beast probably has no use for a bridge. It could just fly over this puny stream using its hideous wings."

He turned his attention back to the troll and saw that he was shaking. "Are you scared?"

"What?" Boggwyn said, his fingers still in his ears.

"Are you scared?" Snarly repeated.

"Area rug?"

Snarly sighed. "No—"

"What about an area rug? I have been looking for one."

"I didn't say anything about an area—"

Boggwyn smiled broadly. "Do you have one? I could buy it from you."

"I didn't say—"

"I don't have any money, but I have *lots* of mud."

"Take your fingers out of your ears!"

Boggwyn looked confused. "Make a V-neck out of bird hairs? I don't think that would be very comfortable."

"Will you—!"

"Not very comfortable at all."

"Unplug your ears!"

"A pug for fears? Ah, yes, that certainly would make *me* feel calmer."

Snarly put a hand to his forehead.

"But the real question is, what's a pug? And where can I get one?"

Snarly motioned with his hands. "Take your *fingers* OUT of your *EARS!!*"

Boggwyn finally understood and pulled his fingers out of his ears, bringing thick strings of smelly earwax with them. "Oh. Sorry. I forgot I put them there. What was it you were saying?"

"Nothing. Never mind."

Boggwyn shrugged. "Okay," he said, and then picked a bug off the railing of the bridge and ate it.

Snarly narrowed his eyes. "You're not much of a troll, are you?"

"Listen, little person, I don't think you should go into the Black Forest, and I *'specially* don't think you should go to the Pretty Forest to go looking for some *thing* called the Beast.

It sounds really very dangerous." Boggwyn rubbed his chin, thinking. "I know! Why don't you forget about your little idea of dying and instead come under the bridge with me and have a nice cup of stale river water?"

"No," said Snarly. "I must be going. It was a lovely conversation, really, but if you'd now kindly get out of my way, I'd greatly appreciate it."

"Okay, but, at least," Boggwyn began, as he tried to find something to say, "at least take a weapon of mine to help you defeat this Beast. You know, since I can't go with you myself. On account of having to guard the bridge, not because I'm scared." He scanned the surrounding area and picked up a rock. "Here you go."

Snarly was not impressed. "It's a rock."

"Yes, but a *hard* rock. You can throw it at the Beast."

"Okay. Thank you," Snarly said impatiently. He put the rock in his pocket. "Will you let me pass now?"

"Certainly." Boggwyn stepped aside and let Snarly continue on his way over the bridge.

"Thank you."

"Farewell, little Snarl. It was nice to have met you!" Boggwyn looked quite sad as he waved good-bye.

Snarly waved but didn't turn around. "Yes, yes. You, too."

Not many people crossed the little bridge at the edge of the Whispering Woods. *Oh well,* thought Boggwyn, and then he crawled back underneath.

As soon as Snarly stepped off the bridge, he took the rock out of his pocket and tossed it back over his shoulder. It made a *plop* as it went into the stream.

Just a couple steps later and he was engulfed in a dark shadow cast by the canopy above. That could only mean one thing: he had just entered...

The Black Forest

(CHAPTER 7)

SNARLY SINCERELY HOPED HE WAS OUT OF THE BLACK Forest before nightfall. It was about the middle of the after-noon, but it looked like night already. That's why it was called the Black Forest, after all, because the trees blocked out the sun during the day, and at night everything was black as pitch. No wonder he'd gotten lost as a child. For all he knew, he was lost now!

Walking around—in what he hoped weren't circles— Snarly was very jumpy as he thought about all the stories he'd heard about this place, stories of poisonous creatures, quicksand pits, and madness-inducing sensory deprivation. And this wasn't even the scariest forest!

He wanted to light a torch, to combat the suffocating darkness, but he didn't really want to know what lurked within those shadows. He already had that creepy feeling of being watched. Not only that, but he also remembered the words of warning from his dream. Brutus had told him not to draw too much attention to himself.

After a couple hours of walking, he noticed a little bit of light up ahead. He thought that would make a great spot to rest and eat. Plus, who knew how long it would be before there was another break in the darkness.

When he stepped into the clearing, which was hidden away from the trail, he had to shield his eyes from the light, even though it was still pretty dim (any amount of light in the Black Forest seemed like a lot), and what he saw took his breath away. Spotlighted, standing before him, was a beautiful fountain, lined with budding vines. The water springing forth was clear as crystal, and its design looked to be made by the hands of—

"Stop right there with your movements, good sir!"

"Ah!" Snarly whirled around. "Who are you?" he asked. But to himself, he thought, *Wow! A real, live centaur!*

The centaur stamped the ground and stepped forward, spear in hand. He towered over Snarly, who was awestruck. "I am Handell, Keeper of the—whoa!"

Snarly jumped back as Handell the centaur lunged forward. "What happened? Are you okay?"

Handell was hopping around, clearly in pain. "I tripped. Stubbed my hoof on that rock over there." He rubbed his ankle. "Twisted my ankle a little, too." He shook it off and stood straight again. "Anyway, I am Handell, Keeper of the...the...a—ACHOO!!" Handell wiped his nose with the back of his hand. "Bless me."

"Bless you."

"Where was I?"

"You are Han—"

"I am Handell! Son of Fawndell, grandson of Tyrell, Keeper of the—OW! What in the world?"

"What?" Snarly asked. "What now?"

"Something just bit me!" Handell said, while rubbing his haunches. "Sorry. Like I was saying...mmm. Man, that really stings. Wow."

Snarly tried to wait it out, but this majestic creature was starting to depress him with his whining. "So, you're Handell—"

At that, Handell snapped to attention. "I am Handell, Keeper of the Fountain of Jubilation! Why comest thou into the presence of the great Fount?" He aimed his spear at Snarly and raised an eyebrow. "Comest thou on behalf of mischief?"

"What? No." Snarly slapped the spear away from his face. "I was passing through, and I saw the light."

"I see," said Handell, who relaxed a little. "Say, what manner of creature are you?" He looked Snarly over with mild amusement. "Never have I seen such as you. You are quite funny looking."

Snarly frowned. "Gee, thanks. I'm a Manicher," he said as he stepped closer to fountain. "My people live on the other side of the Whispering Woods, in Sandwich Town."

(I did explain the whole "Sandwich Town" thing, didn't I? No? Wow. I'm sorry. I've been a little unorganized lately. If it's all right, I'll take care of that now. You see, when it was originally founded, the village was to be called Manich

Town, because of the Manich River and all, but when the villagers commissioned Old Man McFwaddle, who was very hard of hearing, to build them a huge "Welcome to Manich Town!" sign, he thought they said *Sandwich* Town. Well, being a bunch of cheapskates, they decided to just change the name rather than pay for another sign. And that's the story of Sandwich Town! Now let's get back to the story of Snarly and the Beast...)

Handell stepped toward the fountain as well. "Sandwich Town, eh? Sounds yummy." He kept a watchful eye on Snarly, in case he should make any sudden, undesirable movements. "You are a long way from home then?"

"Yes," Snarly said. "What is this, anyway? What's the Fountain of Jubilation?"

Handell puffed himself up, full of pride, and stated, "The enchanted Fountain of Jubilation will grant unconditional happiness to any who are worthy enough to drink of its waters. If you were to take but one sip from this fountain, no matter what ills may befall you, you would forever have a smile on your face."

"Hmm."

"'Hmm?'" Handell stepped back. "Is that all you can muster for such a wonderful relic? *'Hmm?'*"

Snarly circled the fountain. "I've been mean and grumpy my entire life," he began. "Do you really mean to tell me that the water in this fountain can cure me of my destiny?"

Handell struck the ground with the butt of his spear. "The glistening water in this remarkable fountain can change anyone!" Then he walked over to a large, hollowed-out stone and produced an ornate ladle. He held it out for Snarly to take. "If you do not believe me, try it for yourself." He looked Snarly up and down. "I can see how badly you need its magic."

Snarly snatched the ladle out of Handell's hand. He scooped up the gleaming water, sipped ever so gently, and then choked on it.

As he sat on the ground, gasping for air, Handell cocked his head to one side and said, "Hmm. This has never happened before. Very strange."

"What does it mean?"

"Perhaps you have a tiny esophagus. Try again."

Snarly got up and tried another ladleful, carefully, and this time he did not choke.

He looked up at Handell, who said, "Well, how do you feel?"

Snarly didn't smile, though. Instead, he winced, and then burped so loudly that a nearby squirrel dropped her acorn and ran up a tree.

"Very strange," Handell repeated. "Maybe you were right. Maybe you are destined to be grumpy. You are quite a unique individual, uh…"

"Snarly."

"Snarly," said Handell, with a bow. "Your name suits you. I like you, wee one. I shall join you on your travels."

"Don't you need to watch the fountain?"

"It'll be fine. You're the first person I've seen in eleven years. And besides, I will return. I only want to make sure that you safely get to where you are going."

Snarly shrugged. "Okay. I suppose I could use some help navigating this forest."

"Excellent!" Handell exclaimed with the stamping of a hoof. "So, where are we going?"

"I am on a quest to find and slay the dreaded Beast, which dwells in the heart of Pretty Forest."

Handell's entire demeanor changed. "Nope," he said.

"What?"

Handell shook his head. "Nope. I'm not doing that."

"Why not?"

"Because that, my tiny friend, is suicide." He struck the ground with his spear again and stood tall. "I am sorry, but my post is here. For I am Handell, son of Fawndell, grandson of Tyrell, cousin to Syndell, nephew of Yondell, pen pal of Willie, acquaintance of—"

He really rambles on for quite a while here. Maybe we should just move on.

As Snarly continued on through the Black Forest, he saw many strange things. One thing in particular was a very annoying tree. It was an early form of the weeping willow called a sobbing floppy (that particular species of plant has calmed down a great deal over the years).

"Hello there," Snarly said as he approached the tree.

But the tree didn't respond to or even acknowledge him. It just kept sobbing uncontrollably.

Snarly tried to talk over the crying. "Excuse me. I wonder if you could help me. I'm a bit lost."

Still, the tree just moaned and wailed and lamented, its droopy branches shaking.

"Hey!"

Nothing.

"Oh, good grief," said Snarly. "Could you stop crying for two seconds and point me in the right direction? Please?"

What Snarly didn't realize was how hard life was for a sobbing floppy in the Black Forest. There was very little light, and many of the larger trees took most of the water. It was very depressing. But still, this was too much, even for Snarly.

"Thanks for nothing!" Snarly yelled as he walked away, which only made the tree cry all the more.

Night had fallen upon the Black Forest.

Eventually, Snarly had to stop walking. It was just too dark. He was beginning to feel panicked, like he might not ever find his way out. He could barely see his own hand in front of his face, so how was he supposed to know if he was going in the right direction?

Think, Snarly. Think! he ordered himself.

He had the lucky flower out again, gripping it tightly in one hand. He couldn't see it, but he could smell it. He breathed it in once more and started to relax.

He had come to think of this mission he was on as something he was doing for her, that little girl named Jasmine. She had shown him a kindness, so he would push forward, no matter how scary it got, and that small flower would be his reminder as to why he was doing it.

With his senses coming back to him (all but his sense of sight, of course) he decided to make camp. He didn't like it—he would be way too vulnerable—but he knew he didn't have a choice.

First things first, he needed to build a fire. Not only did he need the light and the warmth, but a fire would also (hopefully) ward off any dangerous animals.

And then, as if in answer to these thoughts, a howl rose up in the distance.

But not too distant. Not nearly distant enough.

He made a fire as quickly as he could, and, even though he couldn't see anything in the darkness, he was constantly looking over his shoulders as he stumbled around, trying to find firewood, just waiting for something to jump out and get him.

After the fire was lit, Snarly felt a little better. But it wasn't long, and he heard movement—a rustling of leaves here, padded footsteps on grass there.

He drew his sword. He was frozen in place, eyes wide, trying to see through the dark, ears listening for the slightest sound.

Moments later, a large, black wolf jumped out from the shadows of the trees and into the light of the campfire.

Snarly took a defensive stance, held his sword up.

The wolf didn't attack him, not yet. It stood there before Snarly with its head down, growling, the fur on the back of its neck standing straight up, saliva dripping from its fangs.

As Snarly waited, the growl grew louder. Then the wolf sprang forward, but only a little, just enough to make Snarly take a step back.

63

Snarly held his ground, though, and stared into the eyes of the wolf. He knew he couldn't show his fear. But the wolf kept coming at him, an inch at a time, trying to get Snarly to run.

Finally, apparently tired of waiting for the chase, the wolf howled and lunged at Snarly.

Snarly, of course, screamed and ran the other way. He ran as fast as he could, but he knew he was no match for the wolf. It would only be a matter of seconds, and he would feel the massive fangs sinking into his flesh, only seconds before he would be ripped apart by its massive claws.

But so far, there was nothing. He could still hear the animal running behind him, but, amazingly, it had not caught up to him.

Snarly stopped. The sounds had changed. They were now to his right. Was it another wolf? As fast as he could, Snarly ran to his left, away from the noise.

He stopped again. There were sounds ahead of him now. Were there *three* wolves? What were they doing? Playing with him? Corralling him?

All he could think was *Run, run, run!* So he ran, veering to the right, hopefully away from the wolves, however many of them there were.

He ended up tripping and rolling down a fairly steep hill. Once he reached the bottom, he jumped up, ready to continue running, but standing in front of him, blocking his path, was a small two-story house with a big sign in the front yard. It read...

Ma and Pa Vittle's Bed & Breakfast

(CHAPTER 8)

SNARLY LOOKED BACK, UP THE HILL, AND LISTENED. HE couldn't hear the wolves anymore. He'd lost them!

But still, he ran across the lawn and up the porch of the small house, just in case.

At first glance (and considering the alternative), the B and B seemed nice enough. But nothing could have prepared Snarly for what he was about to see.

He knocked on the front door, and when it opened, he saw the two happiest people he had ever seen in his life. Snarly actually jumped back a little. Their smiles were so big. They were so cheerfully grotesque! Or, grotesquely cheerful. However it should be worded, Snarly didn't know if he would be able to handle it. A thought flashed through his mind—*I'd rather have the wolves!*

"Welcome, stranger!" exclaimed the man.

"Hi?" said Snarly.

"Come on in!"

"Let's get you out of the cold!" the old lady said. She looked so much like a Christmas card, was so jovial, Snarly felt like he might puke.

"But…it's not cold," he said.

Pa laughed and said, "Come on now, don't be shy!" He tried to grab Snarly's arm.

Snarly resisted, saying, "Oh, no, that's okay. I—"

"Don't be silly!" interrupted Ma. "It's late and dark and we have plenty of room!"

"No. No, I don't want to. I—"

But they both reached for him, hands grabbing at his clothing.

"No, please…"

But they had him, and they were pulling him through the door.

"Help me!" Snarly screamed in terror as the polite elderly folks tried to bring him into their warm, sweet-smelling house. "Please! Someone! Anyone!"

He latched on to the doorframe and screamed into the night, "Wolves! You can eat me! Just get me outta here!"

But it was no use. He'd lost his grip. He was inside.

And then, as the door closed: "*NNNOOOOO!!!!*"

The next morning, the sun shone brightly into this sinister, unearthly clearing. Cute little bunny rabbits hopped around playfully, while energetic little birdies cheerfully chirped to each other. The early morning sun tried its best to push little rays of light through the dense foliage, causing the dew to shimmer like tiny diamonds. It was horrible.

Well, not to us. To us, it would have been a very pleasant place, and I'm sure we would all happily give Ma and Pa Vittle's Bed & Breakfast a five-star review. But to Snarly, it was a nightmare.

That night, they ate a wonderful supper and played board games together. They all sat in the living room as Ma and Pa recounted for Snarly all the funny stories they could remember from their life together. And then, as the evening came to a close, they made him a bedtime snack, helped him brush his teeth, and said their prayers while knelt down beside the bed. They tucked him in and gently kissed his forehead, wishing him sweet dreams and playfully warning him of biting bedbugs. They even left the door cracked open, with a nightlight in the hallway.

Snarly laid awake in bed for the longest time, terrified that they might come in again to torture him some more.

Then, when he finally did fall asleep, he had the most pleasant, cheerful nightmares he'd ever had in his whole life.

In the morning, they came in singing, threw back the curtains, and served him breakfast in bed. They packed him a little sack lunch in a brown paper bag, each one writing an encouraging note letting Snarly know how much they loved him and wished him luck on his journey.

It was too much. He was about to go insane. As soon as he got the chance, he made a break for it. He ran out the front door, onto the porch, shielding his eyes from the sun.

But that wasn't the worst part.

The worst part was his face. His poor, poor hideous face.

They had done something to him, changed him some-how. He was…he was…smiling! From ear to ear!

Snarly felt his mouth and collapsed onto the porch.

What have they done to me? he thought, horrified.

Though he was smiling, his eyes were full of fear and panic, and he was sweating profusely.

What do I do?!

He shook his head and rubbed his face as hard as he could—as if trying to scrub away the vilest filth or blackest marks from the most permanent marker—and when he looked back up, it was gone. His familiar, comfortable frown was back.

Oh, thank goodness, he thought. Then, out loud, "No! Not goodness. Thank…thank badness. Thank repulsiveness!"

"Snarly?" Ma called from inside the house.

Snarly clapped both hands over his mouth. Too loud. He'd been too loud! *Fool!*

He could hear them moving toward the front door.

"Don't you mean *Smiley*?" Pa asked with a laugh.

"No," Snarly said as he scrambled backward, down the porch steps. "No."

He got to his feet and took off running, down the porch and through the yard, just as Ma and Pa opened the door.

"Snarly!" Ma called after him. She held up the brown bag holding his lunch. "You forgot your lunch!"

But Snarly didn't care about her perfect little sack lunch. He wanted nothing more to do with these horrible, cheerful people. He'd rather starve!

"NO!!" he screamed, and he ran through the forest as fast as, and for as long as, he could.

Eventually, he found himself at the barrier that separated the Black Forest from the Pretty Forest. It was the huge wall of plants he'd been shown in his dream. On the Black Forest side, the shrubbery was green and full of life, for it was here that the shadows that gave the forest its name began to clear up. But the other half of this natural wall, the half Snarly couldn't see yet, was squishy with decay and smelled of rot.

Snarly pulled the flower from his pocket and looked at it. It was beginning to fade but was still very pretty. He inhaled deeply, held the scent in his nostrils a moment, and then carefully put the flower back and began climbing the wall.

On the green side, it was almost as if the plants were helping him to his destination. He climbed with great ease, which was quite a different feeling for him, what with his short legs and all. He made it to the top quickly, and there he sat, taking in the view of where he'd been. From here, atop the wall, out of harm's way, the Black Forest didn't seem all that scary.

I suppose that's the benefit of hindsight.

But then he looked to his left, and what he saw filled him with dread. His heart sank down into his chest, his mouth went dry, and his legs felt like rubber. He found that he couldn't move, just sit and stare into the abyss. Just sit and stare into…

The Awful, Dreadful, Horrifying, Terrifying...PRETTY FOREST!!
(CHAPTER 9)

AS HE CLIMBED DOWN THE WALL ON THE PRETTY FOREST side, the plants and vines seemed to be pulling Snarly in, almost enveloping him. A giant Venus flytrap came to mind. He hoped there weren't any of those in this forest of doom.

It was a difficult descent—there were thorns, and he had to be careful not to step on or grab a vine that was dead and dry. He winced as centipedes and large ants and other bugs scurried over his hands.

Once he made it close enough to the bottom, he let go and jumped the rest of the way to the ground.

Right away, he got stung by a bee, or something. He swatted at it, tried shooing it away, but nothing worked. The thing just kept coming!

Then he noticed something strange: the bee wasn't a bee at all. It was a flying insect, but not like anything he had ever seen before. It wore a helmet, with tiny holes on top so its antennae could stick out, and the armor had slots for wings. And it wasn't stinging him, it was stabbing him with its tiny sword.

"Hey!" Snarly yelled. "Stop that!" He swatted at the bug again.

The thing looked like it was shouting at him, but all Snarly could hear was a quiet buzzing.

"What?"

The bug clipped a miniscule device to the front of the helmet's faceguard. "State your business!" it demanded.

The device must have been an amplifier, for now the bug's voice, which was probably deafening to it, could now be heard, but just barely, by Snarly.

"None of yours!" Snarly snapped back.

"You are trespassing!"

"No I'm not!"

"State your business!"

"No!"

"Then prepare to die!" The winged bugknight held up its sword and flew right at Snarly's throat. Snarly whipped out his short sword and parried the attack seconds before his throat would have been sliced. (Sure, it would have been a tiny slice, more like a papercut, but, as you know, sometimes the smallest cuts are the most painful ones.)

"Back off!" Snarly yelled as the two went back and forth, sword to sword, striking and countering. Then the bugknight flew back a little, needing to take a breath.

"What's the matter with you?!" Snarly shouted. He was breathing heavily as well, his hands on his knees. The bugknight was small, but he sure was fast.

Instead of answering Snarly's question, the flying nuisance flared a hateful grimace and brought its sword back, ready to strike. It flashed forward, wings flapping fiercely, and then—*PHTT!*—it was gone.

Snarly blinked, confused. "What—"

He shuffled his feet, looking all around, sword at the ready, in case the pesky thing should come flying at him from another direction.

But it didn't. It was just...gone.

"You're welcome."

Snarly jumped high into the air and whirled around. He pointed his sword toward the sound, but all he saw was a huge, fat toad sitting on a log.

It said, "It was amusing at first, but your little swordfight was starting to go on for a while. Thought I'd help put an end to it."

"You—You ate it?"

"Hey, it's what I do. I would have eaten you, if you weren't so big." Then it croaked and jumped off the log. "So, you're welcome." And with that, the toad just up and hopped away.

Wow, thought Snarly. *Brutal place, this Pretty Forest.*

Now, in case you've forgotten, Pretty Forest was probably the scariest place in the entire world. How did it get such a cute name, you ask? Because the one who named it was a giant, insane, homicidal ogre named Goggy Blass. Pretty Forest was his home. That's right, the whole thing.

He named it Pretty Forest to hopefully get more people to come to it…so that he could eat them. Of course, by now, most everyone—except strangers, maybe—knew it was a dangerous place, and they all stayed clear of it.

Being Goggy Blass's home, no one else was welcome to live there, so the fact that this was supposedly where the Beast lived, at the heart of the Pretty Forest, made Snarly wonder what kind of unimaginably horrible creature he was going to be going up against.

As he walked on, Snarly followed an old, overgrown path, and anytime he started to feel nervous or lonely, he would again be sure to pull the flower from his pocket. As he looked at it now, he remembered the little girl, Jasmine, and how pretty she was, just as pretty as the flower she had given him.

Snarly sighed and put the flower back. He didn't need to be thinking such thoughts, not in a place like Pretty Forest. It was bad enough that he was all alone, he didn't need to be distracted, too.

Of course, he had always been by himself, but he had never really been *alone* alone. Not like this. The village was full of people, and he could always hear them. He supposed he'd taken that for granted. Perhaps he should have been a little friendlier, not avoided everyone so much. If so, maybe he wouldn't be by himself right now. Maybe he would have a friend to share in this adventure.

As Snarly thought his remorseful thoughts, he heard something, a sound carried by the wind. He stopped and listened. It was very quiet, and quite far away, but he could hear it, nonetheless.

He held his breath, hoping to hear it better. It sounded like a long, drawn-out roar. Snarly sure hoped it wasn't a dragon, but, this being Pretty Forest, anything was possible.

There it was again! His ears caught hold of the sound and were not letting go.

It sounded as if it was to the north. Or was that west? Snarly was very bad with directions. It was *that* way, whichever it was, and so he cautiously headed in the direction of the ominous noise.

It didn't take Snarly very long to find the source. The sound had sounded far away because it was coming from the inside of a cave.

He thought, *This is it. It has to be. The Beast's lair. The monster's cave.*

Snarly raised a skeptical eyebrow. Odd, though, that it had an address.

There was a walkway leading up to the cave entrance, and at the start of that walkway was a wooden sign. The sign was held up by a cuddly, wooden bear, letting everyone who could see it know that they had reached...

1212 Cuddly Bear Lane
(CHAPTER 10)

ONCE HE GOT A BETTER LOOK AROUND, SNARLY CHANGED his mind. *It looks like the cave from my dream,* he thought, *but this can't be it. It can't be.*

If it was, it had to be a trick, or a trap of some kind.

There was a welcome mat, a lawn gnome, a sprinkler watering the yard. *What kind of Beast would live here?* There was even a sign near the entrance of the cave:

But that sound—which Snarly had by now learned was someone snoring, someone huge, no doubt—*had* to be the

Beast. It must have eaten the people that lived here. And by the look of these lawn furnishings, it must have been an elderly couple.

Snarly decided that he should slay the Beast in its sleep. That would be his only hope for survival. After all, the Beast was probably ten times as big as he was.

He rose to his feet, moved the brush to the side, and was about to step out onto the well-manicured and welcoming walkway, when he stopped.

He couldn't do that. He couldn't kill the creature while it slept. It seemed wrong, somehow, even if the Beast was the cruelest thing to ever walk the earth.

So, Snarly sat back down, leaned against a log, and took a deep breath. He should rest, gather his strength. He would need it to fight the Beast.

And then, Snarly thought, *as soon as it comes out of the cave for its morning kill, that's when I'll strike.*

But how long would he have to wait? It was already almost lunchtime, and this thing was still asleep? What a lazy Beast.

Hmm. Snarly looked around. *Should have brought a deck of cards or something.*

And then he thought he heard the snoring stop. He sat up and listened, his heart beating heavily, but it started back up again.

Snarly relaxed. Never mind. *It must have sleep apnea,* he thought, because it was…

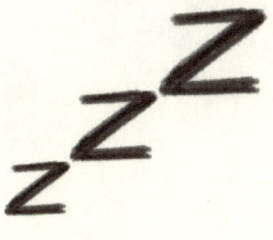

Still Snoring

(CHAPTER 11)

JUST TO GIVE YOU AN IDEA OF HOW LONG THE BEAST SLEPT and just how loud its snoring must have been, I've devoted a whole chapter to it...

Bryan Simpson

Snarly and the Beast

Bryan Simpson

During this time, Snarly nodded off himself and had terrifying dreams about…

Confronting the Beast
(CHAPTER 12)

IN HIS DREAMS, SNARLY SAW THE BEAST AS HE ALWAYS had, from the many legends. It was a hideous creature. And just as it was about to sink its claws into him, the sun rose a little more, and the light found its way to Snarly's eyelids.

He woke up slowly and wiped at the string of drool hanging from his mouth, then sat up quickly as he remembered where he was.

He sighed and relaxed a little.

That snoring—*That dreadful snoring!*—was attacking his ears when he fell asleep, it followed him through his troubled dreams, and now, as he regained consciousness, it seemed to be taunting him, reminding him that it was still there, a monotonous, steady rhythm. But he would endure it, he would wait it out, and he would use it. That incessant snoring was driving him crazy, and he would use that insane rage when it came time to face the Beast.

The question still remained, though: How long was this thing going to sleep?!

Snarly sat on the log and opened up his knapsack. He pulled out the last of his provisions, a slice of apple and a small piece of bread. At least there was time for lunch, small as it was.

But what if the Beast was hibernating? He hadn't even thought of that. Snarly realized then just how little he actually knew about the Beast. The stories were so many, with details so vague and ambiguous, that there really was no clear idea of what the Beast looked like. He supposed he would know a Beast when he saw one.

He imagined it would be a ghastly thing, slimy and dirty, with awful fangs and jagged claws. It would be huge, with grotesque posture, hunched over, dragging itself through the world, always on the lookout for meat, fresh or otherwise. Its snakelike eyes could hypnotize its prey. Its drool was poison, killing the grass and flowers as it oozed from its mouth, like acid. And the stench of its body would—

There! Movement in the shadows!

Snarly hadn't even noticed that the snoring had stopped. He leapt behind the log. Had he been seen? How long had the Beast been awake?

Did it really matter at this point? He needed to attack, now, before he lost his nerve.

Snarly reached into his pocket for the lucky flower, but it was gone! How? He'd carried it in his pocket the whole time. He wanted to go back and look for it, but he knew he didn't have the time. He had come to depend on that flower for comfort, though.

Snarly steeled himself. *It got me this far,* he thought. He didn't like it, but he would now have to go forward on his own and face his fears.

So, he grabbed hold of his short sword and took a deep breath. He tightened his leg muscles, ready to spring into action…but something stopped him.

He squinted his eyes in an attempt to see better. Surely he wasn't seeing this correctly. But he was. Snarly's jaw dropped in shock.

The Beast stepped out of the shadows of the cave and into the sunlight.

And it was nothing like he'd pictured. It was nothing like any of the stories he'd ever heard.

It was clearly the Beast, he had no doubt of that, but it wasn't very frightful.

Then again, Snarly supposed it didn't really matter what a thing looked like. If it was mean it was mean.

It looked sort of like a bear, only larger, and with long, droopy, pointy ears. It walked upright, on two legs, and its fur was an orange color, with darker orange stripes. The eyes gave the Beast an innocent, harmless, almost childlike quality. It had fangs, but they were not dripping with acidic poison. And its claws were not jagged at all, but nice and clean.

As the Beast came out of its cave, it squinted at the sunlight and stretched, cracking its back. It opened its mouth (Snarly thought for sure it was about to roar.) and yawned.

And in its paw—was that a watering can?!

Snarly watched as the Beast shuffled over to the small garden and watered the plants. He furrowed his brow. *What is this?* he wondered. So, the Beast eats an elderly couple... and then tends to their garden? The Beast did not eat vegetables! It was a vicious carnivore!

It raised a fur-covered arm, and Snarly watched in horror as a beautiful butterfly landed on its extended finger.

Now the Beast will show its true colors, thought Snarly. *This disgusting predator is about to eat that poor butterfly!*

As the Beast smiled, showing its gleaming (and surprisingly white) fangs, Snarly couldn't take it anymore. He could not stand by and watch this innocent creature get eaten alive, and so he leapt out from behind the bushes, sword held high. "Halt, Beast!"

"Ah!" The Beast screamed and fell back on its rump. The butterfly quickly fluttered away to safety. "Who are you? What do you want?"

Snarly gave his most authoritative pose and said, "I, Sir Snarles Alabaster Smallbottom, do hereby—what are you looking at?"

"It is pretty small, isn't it?"

"What is?" Then Snarly noticed what the Beast was looking at and narrowed his eyes. "Do not mock me, Beast. Now listen, and listen well." He began again. "I, Sir Snarles Alabaster Smallbottom, do hereby amputate thee from this land, by the power invested in me by the most honorable Mayor Mortimer Mayer!"

The Beast sat with its mouth open, not understanding. "What are you talking about?"

"Just...consider your reign of terror to be over!"

The Beast cocked its head. "Wait. 'Sir?'" It smiled broadly. "Oh! Are you a knight? I've always wanted to meet a knight!"

"Yes. Wait. No. Maybe, I don't know."

Snarly didn't really know how to answer this question. If he said no, that he was not a knight, this Beast would not be afraid of him. Then again, if he said yes, then the Beast would surely eat him, just as it ate all those knights before him.

"All that matters is that I have come to destroy you!"

"Why would you want to destroy me?"

"Because you're evil."

"No I'm not."

"Oh yeah? Then how do you explain *that*?" Snarly pointed at the wooden bear holding the sign. "You did that, didn't you? You woodified that poor little bear cub!"

The Beast cocked its head to the side again. "I what?"

"You used some kind of evil sorcery and turned that bear into wood! Just for your own sick pleasure!"

"I did not!"

Snarly spat on the ground. "You disgust me."

"But I didn't," the Beast said, most sincerely. "I made it. Out of a log. Cute, huh?"

"I also have the note you wrote."

"What note?"

Snarly took the note from his back pocket and cleared his throat. "'Puny villagers, do not send any more knights! Or else! Cordially, The Beast. P.S. Roar!'"

"I didn't write that! I don't even know what *cordially* means."

Snarly wadded up the note and shoved it back into his pocket. "Well, neither do I, but it must mean something pretty bad, coming from a Beast!"

"I said I didn't write it!"

"Probably means 'I'll be eating you soon!'"

"I never saw any knights!"

"Okay, okay, don't bite my head off...which is what Beasts do, as you well know!"

"I think you've got the wrong idea about me." The Beast stood up and dusted off its fur.

"Forget about ideas! Now is not a time for thinking, it is a time for fighting! Prepare to be slayed, Beast!" Snarly charged the Beast, who didn't even move. He slammed into it and then fell to the ground, dropping his sword.

The Beast laughed. "You fell down!"

Snarly got up as quick as he could and kicked the Beast. He slapped it and hit it and then wrapped his arms around its thigh, trying to pick it up so that he could then slam it down, rendering it unconscious.

It was a good plan, though quite unrealistic, and it only made the Beast laugh harder. "Stop it, that tickles. You're tickling my leg!"

Snarly jumped back and then charged again, this time punching the Beast repeatedly in its round belly (which was as high up as he could reach).

The Beast, of course, laughed so hard it couldn't even breath. "Stop! Please!"

But Snarly kept punching. And with each jab, the Beast's plump belly bounced up and down, which was absolutely hysterical to the Beast.

"Look at it!" he cried. "I've never seen it do that before!" The Beast did its best to push Snarly away. "Please. No more. I can't take it, it's too funny!"

Snarly, out of breath, stood on shaky legs as the Beast wiped tears from its eyes. It was also out of breath, but from laughing so hard.

How is it possible? Snarly wondered. That was all he had left in him. He'd given the attack all he had, and this evil creature only laughed at him? He knew he stood no chance whatsoever. He'd have to try a different approach, before the Beast ripped his head off.

He thought of Brutus, begging for food, and decided to take a more diplomatic approach.

"You are a formidable foe, Beast," he said.

"What does that mean?"

"It means that I have found you worthy of my mercy. I shan't destroy you on this day, for on this day you have found favor in my eyes."

"Oh, that's good," said the Beast. "I don't want to be destroyed. That sounds like it might hurt."

"Oh, it definitely would have," said Snarly. "You're very lucky I decided not to unleash my full strength upon you."

"Thank you."

It sure is a goofy-looking thing, Snarly thought. And it was true, this creature certainly was different from everything he'd ever heard about in the legends of the Beast.

"Hey," said the Beast, "does this mean we're friends now?"

"It means we are not enemies."

"'Cause...we could be friends, you know." The Beast looked down at its feet and shuffled the dirt around. "Maybe even best friends?"

"I don't need friends, especially not best friends. And I *especially* especially don't need a vile Beast as a friend."

Snarly had to admit, though, that the Beast was starting to grow on him. It was kind of funny, actually. And it had cute mannerisms, like a pet. Could all the legends be wrong? Maybe this thing had just gotten a bad rap, like him.

"Well..." The Beast thought really hard about this. "Then, maybe, we could be *worst* friends."

Snarly considered this. "Hmm. That might just work. That wouldn't ruin my reputation."

"You have a reputation?"

"Oh, yeah. I'm a big deal back home."

"Really?"

"You bet."

"Wow."

Snarly liked the way the Beast was looking at him. He'd never been revered before. "Plus, it could prove useful, having someone of your size around."

"Maybe we could be *best* worst friends?" the Beast bashfully proposed.

And for the first time in years, Snarly smiled. Like a real, actual, happy smile. It was weird.

"Sure," he said. "Best worst friends it is."

The Beast leapt into the air. "Yay! BWFFs!"

"What does that mean?"

The Beast smiled broadly...

"BEST WORST FRIENDS FOREVER!"
(PART THREE)

WAIT A MINUTE. WHAT? YOU MEAN THE BEAST ISN'T THE horribly horrible creature everyone thought it was?

Wow! What a crazy twist!

Were you surprised? I bet you were surprised. I can picture you now, sitting in a chair or lying on your bed, and you're stunned. You're just speechless, aren't you? I bet you can't wait to turn the page and see what happens next. I bet you're asking yourself, *Am I,* (your name here) *, on the precipice of discovering, through the magic that is reading, the greatest team-up to ever be recorded in modern literature?*

And here I've gone and interrupted the story again.

Ha ha! I HAVE THE POWER!

But don't worry, I won't abuse it. I won't let it go to my head, because I know you're absolutely dying to know...

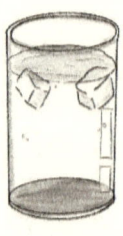

Now What?

CHAPTER 13

AS SNARLY AND THE BEAST LOUNGED IN A COUPLE LAWN chairs in front of the cave, sipping lemonade, Snarly asked, "Why do you live out here in this horrible place, Beast?"

The Beast dribbled a bit of lemonade onto his chin. He wiped it up with his apron, a frilly thing with blue flowers on it. "Horrible? I love it here. I think the Pretty Forest is very pretty."

"Have you ever journeyed very far from your cave?"

"Not really," said the Beast, then gestured with his arms. "I have everything I need right here."

"Then what makes you think it's so pretty?"

"I don't know. Seems nice enough."

Snarly was dumbfounded. "Everything out there wants to kill you! There are wild animals, carnivorous plants. Not to mention Goggy Blass! Who I'm amazed I didn't run into. He's an insane ogre who will kill and eat raw anyone or anything that crosses his path!"

"Well, yeah," said the Beast. "But it's like I always say, if you only look at the negative side of things, then anything can seem bad."

"Who do you always say that to?" snapped Snarly.

"Myself."

Snarly slapped his forehead. "You're impossible!"

The Beast held up a finger. "Nothing is impossible."

"Can you turn into a bowl of soup?"

"I don't think so."

"Ha," said Snarly. "I win." He sat back and drank some more lemonade. "So, now what?"

"What do mean?"

"Well, I was supposed to go on a quest to find and slay you."

"You're not going to, are you?"

Snarly looked at the Beast and sighed. "We're already past that, Beast."

"Oh, yeah. I remember now."

"Say, that reminds me. What's your name? I can't very well keep calling you 'the Beast.'"

"Good," said the Beast (or whoever he was), "because I'm not one."

Snarly rolled his eyes. "Yeah, sure. Anyways, what's your name?"

"Name?"

"Yes, your name. What are you called?"

"Hmm." The Beast thought about it. "Well, no one's ever called me anything before. Except you. You called me 'the Beast.'"

"Your parents didn't give you a name?"

The Beast looked very confused. "Parents?"

"You do have parents, don't you?"

The Beast shrugged. "Not that I remember. Where would they be?"

Snarly stared at him, unbelieving. "You're so weird."

"Thank you. I think."

"Okay," Snarly said, shaking his head, "let's just skip that for now. But you must have a name."

"Why?"

"Because everyone does. Every*thing* does. It's how we know what we're talking about when we're talking about stuff."

"Oh." Maybe the Beast understood this concept, but I'm not so sure. "How do I get a name?"

"Well, since the whole 'parents' thing is a little fuzzy, you should just name yourself."

"How?"

"Just make one up. What sounds good to you?"

Right away, the Beast said, "Food."

"Yeah, food does sound good, but it's not a name. Try again."

"Wibble-wabble."

"That's not even a thing."

"Gloria."

"That's a girl's name."

The Beast thought again. "Super Strongman!"

"I'm not calling you that," said Snarly. "Come on, something simple."

"Hmm..." The Beast tapped his forehead. "How about...Beast? No. No, that's what we're *not* wanting. What if my name was..." He collapsed back in the chair, defeated. "I don't know! Picking a name is hard."

"Well," said Snarly, "let's try it this way. Stand up, let me get a good look at you. Let's see what fits." They both stood up. "So, what is it that makes you *you*?" Snarly stroked his beard. "You're furry."

"Furrious?" said the Beast. "You know, like *fur*ious, but *furr*ious?"

"Yeah, I get it. I don't like it. What else?" Snarly looked him up and down. "You have a definite dirt smell."

"Dirtanian?"

"No. Wrong story," Snarly said. "Being in that cave for so long, you seem pretty ignorant."

"How about Ignoramus?"

"I don't think you want to go there. Trust me. What's a better feature?"

"I don't know."

"You're enormous, I know that."

"Normus? What's 'normus'?"

"Hey," Snarly said as he snapped his fingers, "that sounds good."

"What?"

"Normus. That's a cool name. You like it?"

The Beast considered it. "Yeah," he said. "Normus. Mr. E. Normus, of 1212 Cuddly Bear Lane."

Snarly nodded. "Has a nice ring to it. Now how about a last name?"

"Last name. Hmm. I don't know."

"Well, you'll figure it out."

The two stood there for a moment, their smiles eventually fading. They continued to stand, neither one really knowing what to do next.

Snarly awkwardly clapped his hands together and said, "Well, I guess that's taken care of."

"Yep," said Normus. Then, "So, no one told you what to do after you slayed me?"

"Nope."

"What do you think you would have done if you would have—gulp—slayed me?"

"You don't say *gulp*, you just do it."

"Oh."

"I suppose I would have gone home," said Snarly. "But I don't ever want to go back there again."

"Why not? I thought you said you were a really big deal there."

"I am. I'm, uh, *too* big of a deal for them. They can't handle me anymore."

"Oh, okay. That makes sense." Actually, Normus didn't understand it at all, but he didn't want to admit that to his new friend. Then he jumped as there was a loud rumble, like a thunderstorm in the distance, and covered his eyes. "What was that?"

Snarly laughed. "That was my stomach, you big baby!" he said. "You are a horrible Beast!"

Normus stood tall. "I told you, I'm not a Beast!"

"Oh, yeah? What are you then?"

"I'm a—" Normus began, but then sagged his shoulders. "I don't know."

"I know you're whiny," said Snarly. "Anyway, another thing I know is that we have to have food. I'm starving. What do you eat, Beast—uh, Normus?"

"Bark, grass, flowers, mud—"

"Yuck!"

"Well, what do you eat then?" asked Normus, slightly ashamed of his apparently disgusting diet.

"Oh, have I got some things to teach you. In my village, we ate sizzling snarp-sausage, fresh-baked banomi bread, and the sweetest desserts you could ever imagine."

"Well, then, let's eat that."

"If you don't have the supplies already, my simple-minded friend, then you must have coins, so that you can buy the food."

"How do you get coins?"

"You have to work." Snarly made a disgusted face. "Blah!"

"And work is bad?"

"Oh, it's the worst!" Snarly sat back down in the lawn chair and leaned back. "You see, I'm what you'd call lazy."

"If we don't work, how will we get coins to buy the food?"

"I never said *we* weren't going to work," said Snarly. "Are your legs broken?"

"I don't think so."

"Then *you* can work."

"What will I do?"

"Well, what skills do you have?"

"Skills?"

"Yes, skills," said Snarly. "What are you good at? What can you do?"

Normus thought about it, then smiled. "I can lick my own belly button."

"You're disgusting." Then he had an epiphany and sat up. "I got it. Let me see your scariest face and your loudest roar."

"Why?"

"Just do it. And make sure it's *really* scary."

So, Normus made his scariest face and gave his loudest roar. Then he folded his hands, looking all cute and cuddly again. "How was that?"

"It was perfect," Snarly said as he rubbed his hands together. "You just gotta hold it out a little longer at the end. Stay in character. You know, stay in Beast mode."

"'Beast mode?'"

"Yeah." Snarly gulped down the last of the lemonade (That *was* lemonade, right? But where would Normus have gotten lemons? Best not to think about it at this point.) and stood up. "This plan is gonna make us rich."

"What plan?"

"I'll explain on the way." And Snarly started walking, leaving Normus to have to hurry to catch up.

"Where are we going?" he asked. "Did you figure out now what?"

"Yeah, I'll tell you now what. Now we go scare us up some food."

"Scare?"

"That's right," Snarly said. "You've got a natural talent, my friend."

"You think I'm scary?"

"Let me put it this way, when you roared back there, I almost wet my pants."

"Really? Wow. I made you almost pee?"

"Yeah, you did." A devilish, diabolical smile flashed across Snarly's face. "There's gonna be a lot of people doing a lot of extra laundry while we're around."

"What do you mean?"

Snarly shook his head. "Never mind. Just get yourself ready to be scary."

"What exactly are we going to do?"

Snarly laid out the plan for him: They would hide behind a tree, or something, on the side of the road, and when a carriage rode by, Normus (AKA the scary Beast) would jump out, claws and fangs glinting in the sunlight, and roar and slash at the air. The passers-by would then be so terrified that they would most likely soil themselves and then run away, screaming and crying, leaving all of their possessions behind.

"But, why would I want to pretend to be the Beast if I'm not?" Normus asked.

"Fear," Snarly said, with a sly grin. "With fear, you can make people do things, things they wouldn't normally do."

"That doesn't sound very nice."

"It's not supposed to be nice. It's supposed to be scary." Snarly stopped walking and looked around. "Is there not a road around here somewhere? A beaten path? Something?"

"There's a road way back over there." Normus pointed back in the direction they'd come.

"Why didn't you tell me we were going in the wrong direction?"

Normus shrugged. "I—"

"Come on."

So, Snarly and Normus turned around and started walking back toward the road, where Snarly hoped to find…

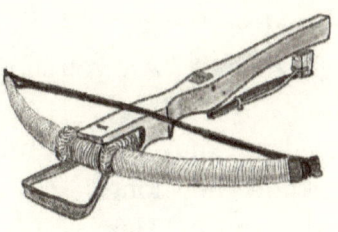

Their First Victims

(CHAPTER 14)

NORMUS RAISED HIS HAND AND ASKED, "AND WHAT DOES *waylay* mean again?"

They had now reached the old road, where Snarly was trying to find just the right spot to play out his dastardly scheme. He sighed. He'd only gone over this plan five times already. "It means you lay...in the way...of where the people are going."

"Oh. Okay." Normus scratched his head. "Why?"

Snarly slapped a hand against his forehead. "So that we can surprise them, catch them off guard, and steal all their goods. I've already explained all this."

"Steal? You didn't say 'steal' before."

"Yes, steal. What did you think we were talking about?" Snarly saw the look of apprehension on Normus's face.

"Don't worry about it," he said. "This is how everyone makes a living these days."

Normus thought about it. "Are you sure? I thought stealing was wrong."

"Oh, what would you know? You've been huddled up in that cave for who knows how long."

Normus looked offended. "Hey..."

"Well, it's true, isn't it?"

Normus dropped his head. "Yeah."

So sensitive, thought Snarly. But he wanted to stay on Normus's good side. "Look, I'm sorry. What I meant was, of course I'm sure. Now come on, we've got to get ready."

It didn't take long. They weren't even ready yet when they heard someone approaching.

"Listen," said Snarly. "Sounds like a carriage."

He and Normus stood in the middle of the road, listening, and, sure enough, a pair of horses came trotting around the bend, slowly pulling a carriage.

"Ha! Our first victims!" Snarly shoved Normus into the tree line beside the road. "Go, go, go," he said in a loud whisper. "Hurry, before they see us!"

Snarly was smiling broadly, but Normus thought there was something a little off about that smile. He looked crazy.

"You ready?"

Normus shrugged. "I don't know if I can do this."

"You have to. We already went over this. We need food and money."

"Yeah, but—" He looked like he was on the verge of tears. "Isn't there another way? I don't want to steal."

"Okay," said Snarly with a wave of his hand. "Well, it was nice meeting you."

"What?"

"I should probably get going."

"Why?" asked Normus. "I thought we were going to waylay."

"You don't want to waylay. And that's fine, but I don't think I can be best worst friends with someone who won't even at least *try* the things I like to do." Snarly shook his head, feigning disappointment. "We just don't have anything in common." And then he lowered his head and started to walk away.

Normus grabbed him by the arm. "Oh, please don't go! I'll try to waylay, I promise! Who knows, I might even like it. Just stay. Please?"

Snarly pretended to think about it. "Okay. I guess I can give you another chance." He pointed toward the road. "Now hurry, they're here. Let's see what you got."

Normus gave him a big thumbs up. "You got it, BWFF."

Snarly rolled his eyes and shooed him out toward the road.

Normus gathered up every ounce of courage he had and jumped out onto the road in front of the carriage. The two horses stopped immediately and whinnied frightfully.

Normus sucked in air until his lungs could hold no more, summoned up all the ferocity he could muster, and let out the deepest, loudest, scariest roar he had ever heard anyone make. He didn't even know he was capable of such a thing.

He supposed Snarly's friendship was just that important to him.

The horses seemed genuinely afraid, but they were so well-trained that they didn't even try to run. And there was no movement whatsoever from inside the carriage.

Normus held his scary stance, though, with his arms in the air and his mouth wide open in a grisly sneer, not sure what to do next.

Snarly stepped out onto the road, looking at the carriage, unsure what to make of it. "Uh...what happened? You didn't give them a heart attack, did you?"

"I your hoe nowd."

"What?" Snarly looked up to see that Normus was still frozen in Beast mode. "You can relax now, weirdo."

Normus put his arms down and licked his lips. "I said, 'I sure hope not.'"

"Well, I guess we better check it out," Snarly said as he stepped up to the carriage.

"Careful!"

"If anyone was in there, they would have come out by now, dummy."

But when Snarly opened the carriage door, there was somebody in the carriage. Two somebodies, to be exact. And they each had a crossbow pointed at Snarly's face.

"Well, howdy-howdy," one of them said with a smile. "And just what do we have here?"

"Oops," Snarly said and smiled back. "Wrong carriage. Sorry 'bout that." He tried to shut the door, but a booted foot stopped him.

"Not so fast there, little guy."

Snarly stumbled back as the two men stepped out of the carriage. When they saw Normus, one of them said, "My, he's an ugly one, ain't he, Pete?"

"Oh yeah. You said it, Turtle. Ugly as sin."

Snarly gasped. "'Mad' Pete McDuffy and Teddy 'The Turtle' Turtlebaum?"

Pete grinned, flashing his (fool's) gold tooth. "The one and onlies," he said.

"You heard about us?" asked Turtle.

"Heard about you?" said Snarly. "Heard about you? Of course I've heard about you! You're the Nasty Rotten Boys, the most infamous outlaws in the land."

Pete was clearly impressed. He rested his crossbow on his shoulder. "So, you heard stories about the two of us, all the way out here?"

"Sure! And, actually, I live way over on the other side of Whispering Woods."

"I never heard of you," said Normus.

Turtle looked back up at Normus. "What in the world is that thing, anyways?"

"That's...no one," Snarly said. "It's nothing."

Normus sat down in the middle of the road and crossed his arms. "You're nothing," he said, pouting.

"Say," said Snarly, "Who's driving your carriage?"

Turtle slid his thumbs under his suspenders. "Well, you see, that there's one o' them new-fangled smart carriages. You just tell the horses where you wanna go, and they go."

"Wow."

"Yep. Stoled it off a couple o' folks just down the road a piece." Turtle snapped the suspenders. "Pretty, ain't she?"

"You bet she is!" Snarly was overflowing with excitement. He said, "Hey, if you've got the time, I sure would like to hear about some more of your robberies! Like, which one's your favorite? And which one got you the most loot. And which one was the most dangerous!"

Pete narrowed his eyes. "You know what? I got a better idea. What's your name, little fella?"

Snarly's eyes glistened with admiration. "Snarly Smallbottom, sir."

"Nice outlaw name," said Turtle.

Snarly blushed. "Aw. Thank you."

"Well, Mr. Tinybottom," said Mad Pete with a big ol' smile, "since you're such a big fan of ours—and you seem to have a real mean streak about you—I think, instead of *telling* you about one of our robberies, how's about we let you be a part of one? What do you think, Turtle?"

"Why, I think that's a grand ol' idea, Petey."

"Really?" Snarly said. "Me? You want *me* to help *you*? With an actual Nasty Rotten Boys robbery?"

"Absolutely."

"Wow." This was a dream come true for Snarly. He'd read all about the Nasty Rotten Boys, knew of all their exciting escapades, their crossbow-toting ways, their hold-ups and robberies and years of running from the law. "What do you want me to do?" he asked.

"All you gotta do, partner," said Turtle Turtlebaum, as he smiled and raised his crossbow, "is reach for the sky."

"Not another word."

"But—"

"I mean it," Snarly said. "Not a word."

Normus held it in until he could hold it in no more, then he burst out laughing.

"Laugh it up, hairball, but I had everything in that knapsack. Now I have no clothes, no canteen, nothing to light a fire with. Nothing. They even took my short sword."

Normus was laughing so hard he couldn't breathe. He managed to get out sentence fragments between gulps of air. "I'm sorry…really…but…they said…and you thought they meant…'I get to help?'…'Reach for the sky!'"

"Yeah, it was hilarious," Snarly said. He kicked at the dirt. "You gotta admit, though, those guys are pretty smart to travel through the Pretty Forest. The law would never expect anyone to come here. It's way too dangerous."

Normus tried to say it with a straight face—"Not so smart for you, though!"—but he started laughing again.

Snarly just stared at him until he calmed down.

Normus could tell Snarly was not very happy with him, so he stopped laughing and cleared his throat. "Sorry."

Snarly eased up on the death-stare and started walking again.

"So, what do you think I did wrong?" asked Normus.

"Ah, it wasn't you. My plan was flawed. It just needs a little revising. Always have a Plan B." Snarly looked toward the horizon. "We'll figure something out."

Maybe, but not before Snarly's world would be turned upside down, yet again. For he wou—

Wait. Hold on.

So, would his world be right-side up now?

'Cause it was right-side up to begin with, then it got turned upside down when everyone voted for him to leave his home and go search for the Beast, and now—

But what's the count at this point? How many times has his world been "turned upside down?"

You know what? It doesn't even matter. It's just a figure of speech. It doesn't literally mean that his world is spinning around in circles, a half-circle at a time.

One could still safely say that his world was turned upside down, each time, and it mean the same thing.

Right?

Sure.

Anyway, Snarly's world was about to be turned upside down. For he would soon discover...

A Terrible Secret

(CHAPTER 15)

"NORMUS, I THINK I KNOW WHAT WENT WRONG WITH THE waylay," Snarly said. "It's all about picking the right targets. That last carriage just wasn't the right one. We need to be wiser about our selections."

They were walking through the Pretty Forest, going no-where in particular, just trying to figure out where to go and what to do next. Snarly didn't even realize it, but he wasn't at all scared or nervous anymore. Having Normus the Beast around made him feel pretty safe.

"It wasn't because they had weapons and were smarter and meaner than us?" Normus asked.

Snarly raised an annoyed eyebrow at him. "Well, it doesn't matter, anyway" he said. "That was just a practice run."

"Oh. So, when do we do a real waylay?"

"Soon." He put a hand to his belly. "First, we gotta get something to eat. I'm starved!"

Normus looked around. "These are some nice-looking leaves," he said as he picked a few. "We could sprinkle some dirt on them, maybe find some mushrooms and squeeze the juice out of them."

Snarly looked disgusted. "That's not food!"

"Sure it is," said Normus. "It's a...dirt and...shroom-juice salad."

"That's not a thing. You just made that up."

"Well, what else are we supposed to eat?"

Snarly looked around. He smiled as he spotted a nest, high up in a tree. It was a very large nest. "Graybird eggs."

"Graywho whatseggsits?"

"Graybird eggs. Very big. Very delicious. Wait here." Snarly started for the tree. "Better yet, get some firewood."

"You're gonna eat baby birds?"

"They're just eggs!" he yelled back, over his shoulder. "Get the wood!"

Snarly climbed the tree, which wasn't too hard—he was fueled by hunger—but when he got to the nest he was surprised to find that the eggs had already hatched...and they were not gentle graybirds.

He sat on the branch next to the nest, his eyes wide. "Vulchars," he whispered.

"What?!" Normus yelled from the ground.

Snarly twisted his body around to face Normus. "Shh!"

The vulchar chicks were asleep, and Snarly wanted them to stay that way. Had they been awake, Snarly would have been very promptly eaten, and that would have been the end of this little story. Close the book. Roll the credits. The end. No, these were not cute, fluffy graybirds. These were giant birds of prey.

"What's wrong?" Normus yelled.

Snarly motioned for Normus to be quiet. "It's a vulchar nest."

"What's a vulchar?"

"Will you—" But Snarly heard movement behind him. He slowly turned around.

All three vulchar chicks were curiously cocking their heads at him.

Snarly swallowed hard. If he climbed down fast enough, he thought, maybe he could get away. They were still in their nest, after all. He could just hurry down before the mother—

Oh boy.

It just dawned on him—how could he have forgotten?!—vulchars didn't build their nests in trees. Their nests rested on top of their heads! (Vulchars had no feathers on their bottoms; therefore, they couldn't keep the eggs warm by sitting on them. It was better to just let the warmth of the sun take care of it.)

As Snarly remembered this key fact, he watched in horror as the vulchar nest rose high into the air. Then mother slowly turned her head, all the way around, like an owl, to face him. She crowed loudly at the sight of the intruder.

There were so many leaves, Snarly hadn't even noticed the huge bird nestled in the group of trees, perched on a lower branch. His hunger had blinded him. The poor guy was so scared, he could barely get out more than a whisper. "Normus. Run."

But Normus was already gone.

Coward, thought Snarly.

Then he lost his grip on the branch completely when the mother vulchar reared her head back and crowed again. He fell all the way down, hitting every branch on the way.

When he hit the ground, he looked back and saw that she had already descended from the trees and was slowly making her way toward him. The nest teetered on her head as the chicks inside gleefully hopped around, knowing their next meal was only moments away.

Snarly's side hurt, and he'd gotten the wind knocked out of him, but he sat up quick and started scurrying backward.

The mother vulchar never took her eyes off of him. When she got close enough, she lowered her head and shook the nest from side to side until the little chicks—which were as big as Snarly—finally got the message and hopped out. She nudged them toward Snarly with her huge beak.

Snarly realized she was teaching them to hunt, and he was the prey!

He got up and ran as fast as he could, but the mother flew up into the air with a single flap of her wings and dropped down in front of him. Snarly fell and stumbled back. Then she lowered her bald head, snapping her crooked beak at him to get him to stay still.

He looked back and saw that the chicks were still coming. Luckily, though, vulchars had long necks, and so the chicks were very awkward runners.

Maybe he could use that to his advantage.

Nope. As soon as he tried to get up, the mother pushed him back down. She flapped her wings, causing the dirt to blow all around, as if they were in the middle of a storm.

She did this until Snarly laid still, covering his face, and then she brought her wings down, surrounding him, forming a sort of pen around him, like he was an animal. (Or like an igloo made of feathers.) There was one opening, one way out, and the three chicks were closing in.

If only I had my sword! he thought.

As they drew nearer, their beaks opening and slamming shut, their eyes full of hunger, Snarly closed his eyes. It was over. There was no way he was getting out of this one.

Then he felt a sudden *whoosh!* of wind—the mother's wings again, no doubt. Snarly waited for the chicks to start pecking him apart, but it never happened.

He opened his eyes, and they were gone!

"What—?"

Snarly looked around and then finally spotted Normus. (It was like one of those hidden picture books—*Where's Normus?*) He was standing in the midst of the surrounding trees, very still, and holding up two branches, trying to pass *himself* off as a tree.

"What are you doing?" Snarly shouted.

"Nothing. Just standing."

"Some help you are!" Snarly stood up and dusted himself off. "What, were you just gonna stand there and watch me get eaten alive?"

Normus lowered his arms. "No. I was, uh, just..." He looked around, trying to find some excuse. "...looking for my...uh...contact lens."

"Contact lenses don't exist yet!" Snarly screamed at him. He started walking over. "What happened? Where'd the vulchars go?"

"I don't know," said Normus. "A big branch just came down out of nowhere and hit them. Knocked them way over the trees." He pointed up and away. "Way over there."

Snarly squinted his eyes, unbelieving. "Nuh-uh. That didn't happen."

"Yes it did," Normus insisted.

Snarly looked around and listened. There was no sign of the devil-birds.

"Hmm. Maybe it did," he said. "A lot of weird stuff has been happening since I started this trip." He waved Normus on. "Come on. As long as they're behind us, I guess that's all that matters."

And so, having very narrowly escaped death, the duo continued on their way. Until they stopped again.

Snarly held up a hand. "Do you hear that?"

"Hear what?"

He turned to Normus and sighed. "If you did, then you wouldn't have to ask."

"So...no?"

Snarly shook his head. "Just follow me."

They headed toward the source of the sound, and as they got closer, Snarly realized that what he'd heard was voices. It sounded like someone was having a party.

When they reached the spot, they made sure to stay well-hidden, and what they found astounded Snarly. The place looked like some fancy resort, only in the middle of the Pretty Forest...and all of the Sandwich Town knights were there!

Snarly watched as those "fallen heroes" played volleyball and horseshoes, or sat reading or painting, or floated in the pool, sipping colorful little drinks with umbrellas sticking out of them and—

"What is this?"

"Do you know them?" Normus asked.

"Yeah. Those are the knights from my village. The ones we thought were dead, killed and eaten by you."

"Normus's eyes grew wide. "Knights? Real knights?"

Snarly slapped a hand across Normus's mouth. "Keep it down," he said in a loud whisper.

"Sorry."

"They're clearly not *real* knights. I mean, they deserted their village for *this*?" He shook his head. "So *they* sent the helmet and the note. I can't believe it."

"Told you I didn't write it."

"Now that I've gotten to know you, Normus, I don't believe you're capable of writing a letter."

"Thank you, Snarly."

"I really can't believe it. They're all here. Maxus, Clotus, Hillengrad. And there's Xavier, getting ready to jump in the pool. Unbelievable."

Snarly stood up.

"Where are you going?"

"I'm gonna give those guys a piece of my mind."

But just as he took a step in their direction, a big spider came down on a web and stopped right in front of Normus's face. Normus got so scared he fell back on the ground with a yelp.

"What happened?" asked Snarly.

"Nothing. I just tripped."

But Snarly saw the fat spider, dangling there, spinning in the air. "Are you afraid of spiders?"

"No," Normus said, defensively, as he jumped back up and dusted himself off.

"It won't hurt you." Snarly went over and flicked the spider, which landed a few feet away. "See?"

Normus shivered. "That's not the point. They're gross." Looking around, he added, "And now I don't know where it is. Great."

"You never cease to amaze me, you know that?"

"What do you mean?"

"If I was as big as you," Snarly said, "I wouldn't be afraid of anything."

"Well, I guess I just don't seem all that big to myself," said Normus.

"Yeah. I suppose not." Snarly looked back toward the knights and their fancy resort. He sighed but didn't move.

Normus asked, "Are you gonna go give them a piece of your mind now?"

"No," Snarly said. "Probably shouldn't. If they see you, they might try to slay you, thinking you're the Beast." He shook his head again. "Let's get out of here."

Snarly was pretty quiet for a while after that. He walked with his head down, staring at the ground. He was upset about the knights, he missed his bed, and he was starving.

"What's that noise?"

"It's just my stomach," grumbled Snarly.

"No. It sounds like singing."

Snarly looked up. He could hear it, too.

Afraid that it might be one of the traitorous knights, he guided Normus over to the brush along the side of the path, where they knelt down. He raised a finger to his lips, signaling Normus to stay quiet.

But it wasn't a knight at all. It was a young girl, and she was carrying a large basket full of sweet-smelling bread, swinging it and singing as she skipped along:

I'm just an or - phan, or - phan,
Car-ry-ing a load of bread.
It would be so fun, so fun,
To use my bas - ket as a sled.
... But I can't ... be - cause ...
there is ... no ... ice!

Snarly raised an eyebrow and thought, *Not the most creative little thing, is she? But my how that bread smells good.* He looked at Normus, who was watching the girl. *But what about Mr. Goody-Goody? He'll certainly object. Unless...*

"You know, I think the problem with that first target was that they were adults."

"But don't adults have more money?" Normus asked.

"Yes, but they can also beat you up, as we recently learned." He put a hand to his chin. "Hmm. I wonder what the opposite of an adult is."

Normus thought about it. "Oh, I know. A child."

"You're absolutely right," said Snarly. "We should try stealing from a child."

"I didn't say that."

"What a great idea you just had."

"You shouldn't steal from anybody, Snarly, but especially not a child."

This will be better than stealing candy from a baby, thought Snarly. *Where there's a baby, there's a mommy. And mommies can hit. They can hit very hard. No, this, this will be...*

Like Stealing Bread From a Nine-Year-Old Orphan
(CHAPTER 16)

NORMUS HAD HIS FEET PLANTED AND HIS ARMS CROSSED.
"But I don't want to."

"Stop whining," Snarly said. "You are, without a doubt, the worst Beast I have ever seen. All you have to do is jump out there and roar. You're just going to scare her, that's it. I'll take care of the rest."

"I don't know…"

"Just do it!" Snarly yelled. "Do you want to starve?"

"But what if *she* starves?"

"She won't," Snarly said. "Children don't need as much food. I'm old. I need more nutrients, or my body will fall apart."

Normus felt very uncomfortable about this. "This is the worst idea you've ever had," he said.

"We've only known each other for five hours! Now go!"

Normus reluctantly walked back over to the spot where they had seen the girl. He looked back once, hoping Snarly would change his mind, but he just motioned for him to hurry up. So Normus jumped out onto the road, looking as ferocious as possible. He roared so loud that the little girl's hair blew back. And just as his roar was winding down, the girl did something that neither Snarly nor Normus could have anticipated: she hit him in the face with her basket.

Normus, taken completely by surprise, did what crybabies do best. He cried, which only confused the girl and embarrassed Snarly.

Snarly panicked. They couldn't let this girl get away. He had to eat, and that bread smelled delicious. He jumped out onto the road and ran up to the girl, trying to look and sound as scary as he could.

"Hold it right there!" he said.

But the girl was about the same height as Snarly, so she wasn't all that scared. She hit him in the face with the basket, too, and he went tumbling down.

"Hey! Watch it!" Snarly yelled at her.

"What do you want?" shouted the girl.

Snarly got up. He held his hands out, to show he was no threat, and slowly walked toward her. "We just want the basket. That's it."

"No way, creep!" the girl shouted and reared back to hit him again.

"Normus!" shouted Snarly. "Quit crying and help me, you big baby!"

Normus wiped his tears away and hurried over.

The girl felt a little more intimidated when it was two against one, but she kept swinging the basket at them as she backed up.

Snarly and Normus kept advancing until they had her backed into a corner. The tall rock wall behind her made it impossible for the girl to get away. Snarly grabbed the basket, but the stubborn girl wouldn't let go.

"Let go!" Snarly yanked as hard as he could, and the handle broke off in the girl's hands. She fell to the ground with a loud *thump*.

With the basket now in his possession (and the girl out of hitting distance) Snarly took off running. He yelled over his shoulder for Normus. "Run, Normus!"

Normus followed his friend back into the woods, but when he looked back his heart sank. The girl, whose name he would later learn to be Tamryn, was sitting on the wet ground, her head in her hands, sobbing. And that was enough to make Normus cry. Again. Seeing the effect their actions had on her, he knew in his heart that...

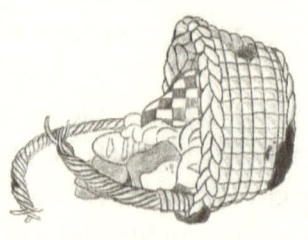

These Spoils Are Rotten
(CHAPTER 17)

"THAT WAS GREAT!" SNARLY JUMPED UP AND DOWN WITH excitement. "Look at all this food! If we're careful this could last us a couple days." He noticed Normus hanging back and shuffling his feet. "What's wrong with you?"

"We scared a little girl and took her food," said Normus.

"I know! It worked perfectly!"

"I think she even got hurt a little."

"And?" said Snarly as he took a big bite of bread.

Normus's chin quivered. "We made her cry."

"So what?" Snarly took another bite and nodded. "This is so good." He handed some bread to Normus. "You gotta try this."

Normus took the small loaf and bit it in half. "So, what if she gets in trouble?" he asked as he chewed. He swallowed the bite and put the rest of the loaf in his mouth. As soon as he swallowed it he realized what he'd just done. "Ah! Oh no! I ate of the stolen booty!"

"It's fine, Normus. You heard her, she's an orphan. She's all alone." Snarly bit into another loaf. "There's no one to punish her," he said through a mouthful of bread.

Normus snatched the basket from him. "How do you know? Just because she's an orphan doesn't mean she's all alone. Maybe she does live with someone, someone who's really mean, who will beat her for losing the food."

"If so, oh well." Snarly tried to take back the basket, but Normus held it above his head. "What can I say? That's life."

Normus gasped. "Snarly! How can you say that?"

"How?" asked Snarly. "It's easy. Watch. 'Oh well.' See? Now you try."

"You're not acting like yourself today, Snarly."

"This is the only day you've ever known me! What's the matter with you?"

"I don't like this plan."

"No, that's not it," Snarly said. "I know what's wrong with you. You're just hungry. If you go too long without food, you can have mood swings and get all crazy. And that's what you sound like right now. Crazy."

"I won't eat any more of this food, Snarly. It's stolen."

"*You* stole it!"

"I know!" Normus threw his hands up and started crying again. "And I'm so ashamed!"

"Don't be," said Snarly. "You have to eat, just like everyone else, right? It's survival of the fittest out here."

Normus set the basket on the ground between them. "If you want to eat this stolen, cursed food, go ahead. But I won't do it anymore."

Snarly snorted and picked up the basket. "Fine with me."

Normus stared at him as he picked through the contents.

"Stare at me all you want, you overgrown hairball. Those puppy-dog eyes won't work on me."

Nope, Snarly wasn't about to let Normus make him feel guilty. No sir. But…he just kept staring at him…staring with those…those stupid, sad, pathetic eyes until—

"Fine! We'll take it back! You big, dumb baby."

"I'm very proud of you, Snarly," said Normus. "This is a big step for you."

"Leave me alone!" Snarly grumbled. "What are we supposed to do for food now? Huh?"

"I guess we'll have to get jobs."

"Oh yeah? And what are *we* going to do?"

"Well, I don't know," said Normus. He looked up into the sky as they walked down the road. "I'm sure there are plenty of jobs for a couple of smart, able-bodied young men such as ourselves."

"First of all, we're not men. I'm a Manicher and you're a Beast."

"I'm not a Beast."

Snarly rolled his eyes.

"And you know what I mean," Normus said.

"Okay, okay. Fine. So what could we do then?"

"We could be…" Normus puffed out his cheeks, thinking real hard. "…bank tellers, delivery guys, tightrope walkers, door-to-door salesmen, cattle rustlers—"

"What are you talking about? We don't have experience doing any of those things!"

"I've always wanted to take up knitting…"

"Just when I thought you couldn't get any weirder," said Snarly. Then he noticed Normus was rubbing his belly. "What's wrong with you?"

"I think that bread was bad."

"I had some, didn't bother me. Maybe it's all that other junk you eat." But then Snarly stopped suddenly.

"What is it?" asked Normus.

"Listen." They craned their necks and could hear talking not too far from where they were.

"What is that?" asked Normus.

"I don't know. Maybe it's the girl. Let's check it out."

They followed the voices and were led to a clearing.

"It's them," said Normus.

"Yeah. And my stuff."

Sitting there, having lunch around a campfire, were the Nasty Rotten Boys. Snarly could see his knapsack and short sword nearby. "All right," he said, "we're going to have to approach this delicately. These are professional outlaws."

He turned around, but Normus was gone. "Normus!" He ducked behind a tree and watched as Normus stomped over to the two bandits. "You dummy," he said, quietly.

"Hey! Look who's back," said Turtle.

"Did you lose your little friend, Fuzzy Wuzzy?"

"The name is Normus. And no, my little friend is hiding behind that tree over there."

Mad Pete and Turtle laughed as Snarly came out from behind the tree. "I wasn't hiding," he said, embarrassed.

Normus pointed a finger at them. "You're not supposed to steal."

"Actually," said Pete, "it's kinda what we do."

"Not today," Normus said. "Give it back!"

Turtle spit into the campfire. "Make us."

Snarly said, "Really, Normus, it's fine. We can find more stuff."

"See, Norm, it's fine."

"No, it's not." Normus turned to face Snarly. "You said it yourself, Snarly, we need that stuff." Then he winced and grabbed his belly, slumping over a little. "Ow."

"What's the problem?"

But Normus couldn't speak. He just looked at Snarly, his face all contorted in pain, and then he started grunting.

"What are you doing?" asked Snarly.

And then Normus—uh—how do I put this—let a windy? Broke wind? Pooted, tooted? Passed gas. However you refer to it, he let it rip right into the campfire, causing a small explosion that engulfed the two rowdy outlaws.

Mad Pete McDuffy and Turtle Turtlebaum let out a couple of shrieks and off they ran to a nearby creek to jump into its cooling waters.

"Ah. That's better," said Normus, with a relieved smile. He turned around. "Where'd they go?"

Snarly looked freaked out by what had just happened.

Then he looked impressed.

Then he gagged and covered his mouth and nose.

"Ah! Gross! It went in my mouth!" he yelled and ran out of the clearing. "Get the stuff!"

Normus shrugged. "Wasn't that bad."

"Feel better now?" Snarly asked Normus.

"Yes. Thank you."

"Just do me a favor and let me know the next time you do something disgusting like that."

"I'll try, but it just kind of snuck up on me."

"And get downwind of me! I don't want it 'sneaking up' on me again." But then Snarly started laughing. "That was pretty neat, though, wasn't it?"

"Yeah," Normus laughed. "Ka-*BOOM!*"

Snarly and Normus had a good laugh, until a scream in the distance caused them to stop dead in their tracks.

One of Normus's ears was raised. "What was that?"

But before Snarly could respond, there was a second scream, and then someone shouted, "I'm sorry!"

"Sounds like someone's in trouble," Snarly said. "That's got to be the girl. Come on."

Snarly and Normus ran toward the sounds of crying and yelling. When they got close enough they hid behind some bushes and saw that it was, in fact, the girl. An old man was yelling at her and hitting her with his walking staff. He was thin and hunched over, wearing a ragged, dirty cloak. He looked weak, but mean, nonetheless.

As the man continued to hit and yell at the girl, Snarly decided he should probably put a stop to it. Sure, he wanted to take her food and leave her all alone and helpless in the Pretty Forest, but that didn't mean he wanted to see her beaten to death by this wacko. So he jumped out from behind the bushes, sword drawn, and shouted, "Halt!"

Tamryn and the old man looked over at him, and neither one seemed to be very impressed.

Snarly knew that could only mean one thing. He closed his eyes and took a deep breath. *What a dumb Beast,* he thought, and turned around to see Normus's cowardly green eyes watching from behind the bushes.

He tried to discreetly motion for Normus to get up and come join him, but the big doofus stayed where he was.

Snarly turned back to the girl and the old man, who were just standing there, looking confused. He offered a weak laugh, then held up a finger and said, "One second, please."

He stomped over to the bushes, looking furious—which only made Normus more nervous—and loudly whispered, "Come on! You're supposed to be backing me up!"

Normus obeyed, but came out timidly, with his head down. "He seems really mean," he said.

"You're the absolute worst, you know that?"

They walked back over toward the girl and the old man.

"I'm sorry, I—"

"We'll talk about this later," Snarly whispered. Then, "Now, as I was saying: Halt! Unhand that child!"

The old man squinted his eyes. His grip on the girl's arm tightened.

"Ow," she whimpered.

"Quiet, girl," he hissed at her. Then to Snarly he said, "This does not concern you, half-man. Take your pet and go back the way you came."

Normus looked back, trying to see what "pet" the man was talking about, then realized the old meanie was talking about him. "Hey," he said with a scowl.

"He's not my pet," Snarly corrected. "And, actually, this does concern us."

The man stood straight. "Don't be a fool, little one. This is family business. Don't try to be a hero."

"I'm no hero," Snarly said. "In fact, I am quite the opposite. We took the food from the girl. We're here now because we're bringing it back."

The old man released his grip on Tamryn, who fell to the ground, and then slowly turned to fully face Snarly. "You stole from me?"

Snarly's mean face lightened up a bit as the man took a step toward him. "Well, we were hungry, and, uh, desperate." He didn't like the look in the old man's eyes. "We made a mistake. And we realize that now. And we're sorry."

The old man pointed a crooked finger at Snarly. "Truly? *You* stole from *me*?"

Snarly backed up a couple steps. "Hey. I said we were sorry. And we brought it all back."

"Well," said Normus and his stupid conscience, "most of it."

Snarly's jaw tightened.

"Most?" asked the old man.

Snarly flashed an angry look at Normus. "Yeah, I guess I kind of forgot about that. We did have a couple bites."

The old man's eyes grew wide. "A couple bites of what?"

"Just bread," said Snarly.

"It was all bread, you fool!" The old man hit the ground with his staff. "From which loaves did you eat?"

"Mine was a soft, wheat bread," said Snarly.

The man pointed at Normus. "And you, creature?"

Normus lifted his eyes. He was so full of shame. "I ate the one that had the little bits of cheese sprinkled on top." He covered his face with his paws and started sobbing again. "And it was delicious!" he bawled.

"Silence!" the old man shouted as he backed away. "You should be dead by now."

Snarly looked at him in shock. "Dead?"

"You've eaten a bread bomb."

"A bread bomb?"

"I think I should like to get behind this tree before you explode into a thousand pieces." The old man started to run away, leaving Tamryn to fend for herself, but stopped suddenly when he heard what Snarly said next.

"A bread bomb. Huh. So that's why your stomach got so upset."

Normus shrugged. "Yeah. I guess so."

"That explains your horrible gas."

"It was pretty bad," said Normus.

"Gas?" asked the old man, as he cautiously crept back toward them.

"Horrible gas," said Snarly.

"This can't be."

"Oh, it was," said Snarly.

"It happens a lot, actually," said Normus.

But the old man wasn't even paying attention to the pair of would-be heroes anymore. "My magic must still be too weak," he said to himself. "There should have been bits of this beast all over the forest."

"Whoa," said Snarly. "What was that bread made of?"

The old man's head shot back to Snarly. "Why, magic, of course."

"No, Papa," Tamryn said.

"Quiet, girl. These two have seen and heard too much already."

"Why would you need magic bread bombs?" asked Snarly, more to himself than to the old man.

"To destroy my enemies, of course."

Snarly gave Tamryn an accusing look. "And you were going to deliver them?"

"I didn't know—"

"Of course the girl didn't know. If she did, she never would have done it. She doesn't have what it takes to blow someone up from the inside."

"But," Snarly said, "what if she had eaten some instead? And blown up herself?"

"Then I would have made more and delivered them myself." Then he added, with a sneer, "That, or I'd find another worthless child to do my bidding."

"Wow," said Snarly, "that's a little *too* mean. Even for me."

"Enough of this." The old man started walking toward Snarly, his bony arms reaching out for him.

Snarly backed up some more. "Okay. Let's all just calm down and talk about this."

"This won't hurt...much. I promise," the old man said with a smile.

"I'm warning you, you psycho. You stay away from us." Snarly tried to look tough, bless his little heart. "You obviously don't know who you're messing with. Don't you know who this is?" he said and pointed to Normus. "Have you never heard of the Beast?"

The old man stopped. He looked slightly amused. "Oh, yes," he said. "I've heard the legends of the Beast. Why do you ask?"

"Well, this is him. This is it. This is the Beast!" He made a grand gesture toward Normus, who waved. "So, you might want to back off!"

The old man chuckled. "You think this puny creature is the Beast?"

Snarly, confused, said, "Yeah."

"The source of all the legends?" the old man laughed. "The source of all the fear and nightmares across the land?"

"Well...yeah. I mean, look at him."

Normus took his claw out of his nose and smiled.

"Look at him? Look at *him*?!" The old man raised his arms high into the air, pointing his staff toward the sky. "Behold!"

"Papa! No!"

The sky turned dark above them as the staff glowed a fierce, deep purple. Lightning flashed from the old man's fingertips and seemed to singe the clouds overhead.

Then he disappeared as a column of leaves began to swirl around him. The column grew taller and taller, and when the leaves and dirt finally settled, the old man stood taller than them all. He towered above them, in fact. He had to be twenty feet tall, at least. He was monstrous, and his eyes glowed that same deep purple.

His voice was as thunder as he bellowed, "Here is your Beast!"

Snarly's jaw hung open. "Oh. Oh wow."

"See!" Normus shouted from behind him. "I told you I wasn't the Beast!"

"Yeah." Snarly could only look up at the monster as it laughed loudly.

"But you didn't believe me, did you! Just kept blaming me for stuff!"

"Uh, Normus—" Snarly said in a quiet voice.

"I bet you believe me now, though, don't you?"

"Now's not the best time for this."

Tamryn ran over. "I have to agree with the little guy on this one."

They all looked up in awe. "What do we do?" asked Normus.

"I have an idea," said Tamryn.

"What?"

"Run!"

The Beast (the real Beast, apparently) threw back his head and howled.

"I think you're right!" And Snarly was gone in a flash.

Normus swept Tamryn up in his arms and ran just as the Beast lunged for them. He ran as fast as he could, but he could feel the crazy old man gaining on them. He could hear the heavy footfalls right behind them, right on his heels, shaking the ground beneath them.

And just when he thought the Beast was about to get them, Normus dropped to the ground, shielding Tamryn.

He closed his eyes and waited for the impact, but it never came. He felt something hit his back, but it couldn't have been the huge monster. It felt more like someone had thrown a broom at him.

Normus opened his eyes and listened, but all he heard was the sound of heavy breathing, and when he looked back, there was the old man, lying on his back on the ground, all thin and feeble again.

Tamryn looked at him and then at Normus. "We have to get out of here, while we still can."

Normus nodded. "Yeah. Let's see if we can catch up with Snarly."

Normus helped Tamryn to her feet and the two hurried away. Normus kept looking over his shoulder, though, thinking that the madman might come to and start chasing them again, but he didn't. He knew they would be no match for the real Beast. They needed to find Snarly, and then they would all have to go...

LOOKING FOR HELP

(PART FOUR)

ANOTHER TWIST?!

I gotta ask, can you handle this? I really do hate to interrupt again, but I feel a certain responsibility to you, the reader. I'm concerned about your well-being. All these twists and turns, the hilarious comedy, the perilous action, the actiony peril. I just wonder if maybe you've bitten off a little more than you can chew.

Maybe you should ask your parents, or whoever, if it's okay for you to continue. I mean, for all I know, you've got a heart condition and shouldn't be on the wild and wacky roller-coaster ride that is *Snarly and the Beast*.

Tell you what, you go ask someone, make sure everything's cool, and I'll just wait right here. Okay?

… … … … … … … … … … … … … … … … … … … …
… … … … … … … … … … … … (whistling while I wait) … …
… …
… … (picking dirt out from under my nails) … … … … … …
… …
… …
… … … … … … (checking my email) … … … … … … … … …
… …
… … … … … … … … … … … … … … … … … … … …

Hey. Welcome back. So what did they say?

Really?

Well, if they're okay with it, I guess it's fine. You're one brave reader, I'll give you that.

Let's move on then and see what else is in store for our motley crew as...

Snarly Explains It All

(CHAPTER 18)

NORMUS AND TAMRYN WALKED FOR ABOUT AN HOUR, AND they still hadn't found Snarly. Normus didn't even know if they were going in the right direction. And how far had he gotten? For such a little guy, with such short legs, Snarly sure could move—if he got scared enough, that is.

"So, what's the story with you and the grumpy guy?" asked Tamryn.

"Snarly," said Normus.

Tamryn rolled her eyes. "Okay, the snarly guy."

"No, his name is Snarly."

Tamryn scrunched up her face. "What kind of name is Snarly?"

"It's a really good name for him."

"So...?" Tamryn nudged. "What's the story with you and Snarly?"

"Oh, we're best worst friends."

"'Best worst friends?'"

"Yeah. Snarly can't have any friends, on account of it'll ruin his reputation. So, instead of having a best friend, I'm his worst friend, his *best* worst friend in the entire world. It's a whole thing."

"Hmm. I've never heard of that before."

"Yeah," Normus said, a little boastfully, "it's a pretty special bond the two of us have."

"I see. Lucky you."

"*Very* lucky."

"And how long have you guys known each other?"

Normus looked at his wrist (there was no watch). "Six hours, forty-two minutes, and thirteen seconds. Fourteen seconds. Fifteen seconds."

"Wow. And your best worst friend just left you behind, huh?"

"Oh, it's okay. I left him earlier. It's how we do things."

"Yeah, he seems like a great guy."

"He is. He's such a big deal, he can't even go back to his own village."

"What does that even mean?"

"You know, I don't know. But it sounds impressive." Normus's eyes lit up. "Hey! You could be our best worst friend now, too. Then we could all go on adventures together and live together, and we could be like a club that everyone wants to be a part of. The Best Worst Friends Club! And everyone would be like, 'I wish I was part of the

BWFC. They have so much fun, and they always look so happy when they're together.' What do you think?"

"I think we need to find Snarly. Let's just worry about one thing at a time. My guardian isn't going to just let me go and forget about me."

"Why do you live with him, if he's so mean to you?"

"He took me in when my parents died. He's all I—"

"*Psst!*"

Normus quickly stood in front of Tamryn, his claws out and ready. "What was that? Is it him? Don't worry, Tamryn. You just stay behind me." And then a rock flew from out of nowhere and hit Normus on the head. "Ow!"

"Over here!"

Normus looked all around, trying to figure out where the noise was coming from, then he saw him. "Snarly!"

Snarly waved them over. "Get off the road. Hurry!"

He led them to an abandoned shack a little ways into the forest, and as soon as they were safe inside, he turned on Normus. "What did you bring her along for?"

"I couldn't leave her behind," said Normus, "not with that mean old man."

"She can't come with us."

"But I've never been friends with a girl before."

"You've never been friends with *anyone* before! Period!"

"True."

Snarly paced around the small room. "You just put a target on our backs, you know that?"

"She needs our help."

"She needs our help. Who's gonna help us?" Snarly yelled.

Then he turned to Tamryn. He looked so angry, she took a step back. "Who was that lunatic? I thought you were an orphan?"

"He's my guardian."

"He's a real piece of work, that guy. Magic? Who is he?"

"His name is Marc Dacaberus."

Snarly froze. "What did you just say?"

"He's my guardian. Marc Dacaberus."

Snarly's face went white, and he fell back into an old, dusty chair. "I can't believe it."

"What? You know him?"

"I know *of* him. And his name isn't Marc Dacaberus, it's Macaberus Darc." Snarly shook his head. He could barely fathom it. "I must say, that's not a very clever alias. He must have wanted to get caught."

"How do you know my guardian?"

"Are you kidding?" Snarly laughed, baffled by Tamryn's ignorance. "Years ago, way before I was ever even born, your 'guardian' was one of the most *evil* sorcerers to ever live. When I was a kid, I read all about him. I idolized the guy. Let's just say, that when it came to being mean and nasty, Macaberus Darc was the master. But then I grew up, and I realized that there was such a thing as *too* much. He wasn't mean in a cool way, he was mean in a scary way. Like, everyone's-gonna-die scary."

"It can't be," said a shocked Tamryn. She knew her guardian was cruel at times, but an evil sorcerer?

"It's true," Snarly said. "I just don't know *how* it can be true. According to all the stories I've ever heard, they both died."

"Who?" asked Normus.

Snarly leaned forward in the chair. He stroked his beard, thinking, and then finally said, "A very long time ago, Macaberus Darc worked as an apprentice for the Great Wizard, Oren Lightenshade. He went by a different name then, of course, one that no one remembers now, but at some point during their time together, Macaberus went dark. He turned from using his magic for good, for helping people, and instead began his campaign of evil, terrorizing the land."

"What happened?" asked Tamryn.

"No one knows for sure," said Snarly. "Some say it was the result of a falling out between the two. Others say a spell backfired on him and caused him to go mad. But it all led to an epic battle between two very powerful wizards. They were thought to have destroyed each other, which is what I always assumed happened."

"So how is he here today?" asked Tamryn. "How is he my guardian?"

"I don't know," said Snarly. "Depends on who you ask, I guess. It's been rumored that Lightenshade simply stripped Darc of all his power and banished him, and that Darc's been rebuilding his magical strength. But if that's true, where's Lightenshade?"

All three of them sat quietly for a moment, none of them knowing what to say.

"All this time," Snarly continued. "All this time, he's been out there, moving in the shadows, getting stronger. And instead of realizing that and stopping him, people invented the story of the Beast." He sat back in the chair.

"What do we do now?" asked Normus.

"We're going to have to get help," said Snarly. "He must be stopped, but he's way too powerful for the three of us. If only Oren Lightenshade was still alive, he would take care of this real quick."

"Well, how do we know Lightenshade didn't survive?" asked Tamryn. "Maybe he's out there, too, just like Darc, trying to get stronger."

"No. If the Great Wizard was alive, we'd know about it. He wouldn't stay hidden from us. He would help us."

"So, do you know anyone else who can help us?"

Snarly thought about it. "Maybe. But we should go ahead and camp out here for the night. I don't want to be walking around out there and run into Macaberus Darc in the dark. We'll leave first thing in the morning."

They all got as comfortable as they could in the old house, but even if they would have had the softest beds, with the fluffiest pillows, they still wouldn't have gotten much sleep. They all laid there, on the floor, listening, expecting Macaberus Darc to show up and finish what he'd started. But all remained quiet, and, eventually, they each nodded off, one by one.

Snarly laid there the longest. He was trying to formulate a plan, and he thought he had one, weak as it was. He would wake Normus and Tamryn up at the break of dawn, and they would head out. He figured, as his first step, he would try to pay...

A Visit to Some Old Friends

(CHAPTER 19)

WHERE ARE WE GOING?" NORMUS WHINED.

"You'll find out when we get there," Snarly said. "Now be quiet so I can think about what I'm going to say to them."

"Say to who?"

"Will you be quiet?"

"You know," Tamryn spoke up, "I would kinda like to know where we're going, too. I don't like taking the time to go somewhere if I don't know where I'm going. Plus, it feels like it's taking forever, because I don't know if we're almost there or if we've still got hours to go or—"

Snarly whirled around to face them. "Okay! Fine! If it will keep the two of you quiet, I'll tell you. I didn't realize it was such a big deal! Good grief! You want me to be the leader, but then you—"

"No one said you were the leader," Tamryn said.

"What? What are you talking about? Of course I'm the leader," Snarly snapped at her. "If I'm not the leader, then who is?"

"I didn't say you *weren't* the leader. I was just saying—"

"What? What were you 'just saying?'"

"It goes without saying that you're the leader," Tamryn said. "Okay? No one's disputing that. It just sounded like you were kind of shoving it in our faces for a minute there, when, technically, no one officially appointed you—"

"I'm not shoving it in anyone's face. Okay? I'm just trying to think."

"Okay," said Tamryn. "Forget I said anything."

"Gladly." Snarly sighed, exasperated by that ridiculous conversation. He started to walk again, but then Normus spoke up.

"Wait a minute," said Normus, "I remember this place. You're going back to those knights, aren't you?"

Snarly sarcastically applauded him. "Yes. Very good, Normus. You figured it out. Now can we continue, please? Preferably in silence!"

"You know some knights?" asked Tamryn.

"Yes, I know some knights."

"From where?"

"From my village."

"Why didn't you just get them in the first place?"

"Because," Snarly said, "they were already sent to slay the Beast, but they apparently had better plans. They walked out on us, abandoned the village they swore to protect."

"What makes you think they'll help us now?"

"Once they know who the real Beast is, that Macaberus Darc is back and getting stronger, they'll help us. I'm sure of it."

"How can you be so sure?" asked Normus. "If they didn't do their job in the first place?"

"Because they're knights," said Snarly, "and even though they may have lost some of their faith in themselves, deep down, they'll know what must be done. Trust me. Now come on."

They arrived at the edge of the clearing where Snarly and Normus first saw the knights. Their little haven was just ahead, beyond the tree line, and Snarly could hear them in there, having their fun, living their good lives. He knelt down and peeked through the trees. Sure enough, they were there, playing volleyball, just like before. Snarly grunted his disapproval at the mere sight of them.

Tamryn knelt down next to Snarly and raised her eyebrows. "These are your great knights?"

"They're the best we've got," Snarly said. "Unless you've got a better idea?"

Tamryn sighed. "No."

"Didn't think so."

Tamryn watched them play volleyball for a second, then made a face. "They're not very good, are they?"

"No, but we're not going to be challenging Macaberus Darc to a game of volleyball."

"That would be awesome."

Snarly flashed Tamryn a disapproving glance. "It's going to be a fight," he continued. "Quite possibly a fight to the death."

149

"And these knights are good fighters?"

"Once upon a time they were. I guess we'll just have to see if they still have it in them." Snarly stood up and looked at his mismatched partners. "Maybe you two should let me do the talking."

"Why?" asked Normus.

"Because they know me. And they'll probably kill you."

"Oh."

With that, Snarly stepped forth. Tamryn and Normus stayed close to each other as they followed a few feet behind. They were all very nervous, which only seemed to get worse with every passing second, and so far no one had even noticed them.

Then one of the former knights looked up and saw him, and Snarly's heart stopped beating. He froze. Tamryn and Normus almost walked right into him, then they froze too when they realized they had been spotted.

Snarly couldn't help but wonder what their reaction might be. Would the knights be suspicious of the trio and lock them up? Would they want to keep their terrible secret and chop their heads off in order to keep them from talking?

It was Maxus, the third knight who was sent to slay the Beast, who saw them first. Snarly was about to turn around and run away, when Maxus smiled at him and waved.

"Snarly, old friend! What brings you to this neck of the woods?"

Old friend? Snarly thought. Such strange behavior for a knight. They didn't seem to be anything like the warriors Snarly once knew. The knights were always too good to talk to commoners like him.

"Um…" Snarly cleared his throat. "Hello there, Maxus. Long time no see."

"I'm surprised to see you all the way out here," Maxus said. "You haven't come to spy on us, now have you?"

"No!" Even though Maxus was obviously joking, Snarly jumped back and covered his throat. "I mean…no. Ha ha."

"Well?" Maxus said. "This is a very dangerous place. So, how *did* you and your friends end up in Pretty Forest, of all places?"

"We have, uh, come to ask for your help," Snarly said.

"Our help, you say?"

"That's right."

"Well, that might be a problem."

"Why is that?"

Maxus held his arms out, apologetically. "Because we're all out of the helping game, I'm afraid."

"Out of the helping game?" Snarly repeated. "What does that mean?"

"It means we're tired of helping."

"Tired of helping?" Snarly couldn't believe his ears. "What does *that* mean?"

Maxus put a hand on Snarly's shoulder. "It's a thankless job, my friend. We've all decided to live out the rest of our lives for ourselves. We're retired!"

"But—" *Of all the selfish—*

Their conversation was interrupted by some of the other knights, who were walking over, having recognized their former neighbor.

"Snarly!" said Clotus. "How have you been?"

"Looking as small as ever, I see," joked Hillengrad.

151

"Yes, yes. Very funny." But Snarly was not laughing.

"Oh! Still grumpy!" laughed Sandurn. "Good for you!"

Hillengrad began to sing loudly: *"Snarly, Snarly, always the grump. Snarly, Snar—"*

"Listen!" yelled Snarly, cutting them off. "Macaberus Darc is back. And he's regaining his magical strength."

Sandurn stepped forward. "Macaberus Darc, you say? Well, that is terrible news, isn't it?"

"Yes. It is."

"I should say it's horrible news," said Dollin.

"Awful news," said Reganstern.

"You're sure of this?" asked Clotus.

"Yes." Snarly pointed to Tamryn. "This girl, she's an orphan. She was raised by Darc. He's disguised himself as a decrepit old man, but there's no doubt. It's him."

"It's true," said Tamryn.

"After all these years," said Dollin. "Amazing."

"Too bad Oren Lightenshade isn't still with us," said Sandurn.

"Aye," said Reganstern. "He would have made quick work of that monster, I'm sure."

"So, you will help us?" asked Snarly.

Maxus shook his head. "No can do, Snarly."

"Why not?"

"Because we have taken a new vow," said Clotus, "one that prohibits us from helping others."

Snarly couldn't believe what he was hearing. "I can't believe what I'm hearing. This is unbelievable. Who are you guys?" He pointed at Normus. "I mean, look here. This is the Beast you were all sworn to kill! Don't you have any urge to get up and fight? Don't you want to take out your swords and cut its ugly head off and pull out its innards and make a rug out of it or something?"

Normus's eyes were wide. "Uh, Snarly? Maybe you shouldn't give them any ideas."

"This is no Beast!" cried Hillengrad. "This is just a big, dumb animal!"

"What?" said Snarly. "Look at him. He's huge!"

"He is large, yes, but we have fought and slain dragons as big as castles." Maxus smiled as if he felt sorry for Snarly for being so ignorant. "This is surely a jest."

No, thought Snarly, as the knights stood there, laughing at him, *they haven't changed a bit.*

"You're a jest," Snarly said under his breath. To Tamryn and Normus, he said, "Come on, guys, let's get out of here."

And then the hapless trio turned and walked back into the Pretty Forest...

Alone and Vulnerable
(CHAPTER 20)

SNARLY DECIDED THEY WOULD HAVE TO LEAVE PRETTY Forest as fast as possible. They would stop for nothing. He also wanted to take a different path, one that would not take them near Boggwyn the troll or Handell the goofy centaur. He'd had enough of them to last a lifetime. He just wanted to find a safe place and live out the rest of his life, hiding from Macaberus Darc and avoiding everyone else.

Tamryn was trying her best to keep up with him—he was walking very fast, clearly angry. "So, what do we do now?" she asked, a little out of breath.

"I have no idea."

"You have to have *some* idea."

Snarly turned on her. "Why? Why do *I* have to have some idea? I already tried to get help, that's all I can do. I'm no hero!" he shouted and kept walking.

"You're all we've got," said Tamryn, quietly, sadly.

Snarly stopped. "Look," he said, "I can't go up against Macaberus Darc. I'm nobody. I'm just a short, old manure bagger from Sandwich Town."

"Your village is called Sandwich Town?"

Snarly closed his eyes and sighed. "It's a long story."

"You make a lot of sandwiches there?"

"No," he said, and tried to walk away.

"Or are you saying Sand *Witch* Town? Like witches that live in sand, or witches that are made of sand?"

Snarly faced her. "No, it's Sandwich Town, like, as in a sandwich, that you eat." He started to move on again.

Tamryn was not getting it. "Well, if it's not known for its sandwiches, then why—"

"Ah!" Snarly threw his hands into the air. "I said it was a long story because I didn't want to talk about it! It's actually not a long story, it's a dumb story! It was supposed to be called Manich Town. Someone messed up the sign. The end." He started to walk away but then turned again and added, "And no, you can't get a decent sandwich anywhere there!"

"Why didn't they just get the sign remade?"

"What does it matter?!" Snarly yelled and stomped off.

Tamryn looked at Normus, who shrugged, and then they hurried to catch up to him.

As they were walking, Tamryn remembered something Snarly had said. "Hey. You said before that you idolized Darc, right? That you read all about him and listened to all the stories."

"Yeah. So?"

"So, that kind of makes you our expert then, doesn't it? If anyone's going to know how to stop him, it's gonna be you!"

Snarly sighed. "It's not that simple. I don't actually know him. I just know stuff about him."

"Okay," Tamryn said, trying to steer him in the right direction. "Stuff. Like what kinds of stuff?"

"Just a bunch of useless information. Nothing that could possibly—" He stopped. Now he was remembering something. "Hmm."

"What?"

"Well, from what I know of that final battle, Darc's wand was broken," said Snarly. "That's how Lightenshade, who was also already weakened by that point, was able to deliver the final, fatal blow. And then, after the battle, the pieces of the wand were retrieved from the rubble at the site of the encounter, and those pieces were supposedly thrown into a fire and destroyed. If he's getting stronger, that means he may have fashioned a new wand. And most likely disguised it, so no one would be suspicious of him."

"His magic is in the wand?" asked Normus.

"Yeah. That was how he controlled it, directed it."

"Okay!" exclaimed Tamryn, but then quickly lost her enthusiasm when she realized she didn't really know how that helped them. "Okay. Now, what do we do with that information."

"That's how the strongest magic must be channeled," Snarly said. "Through a wand. Otherwise, it can become too powerful, even for the one casting it. Tamryn, have you seen anything that might be helpful to us? Anything that you think could possibly be a wand."

"No."

"Think about it," Snarly said. "Be certain."

She thought long and hard. "His walking stick," she said. "It must be his walking stick, his staff. Nothing else does he keep so close, at all times."

Snarly clapped his hands together. "Then that's what we'll need to get our hands on," he said.

"How?"

"I'm not sure yet. First, I think we should go back to my village. At least there we'll have shelter for the night. And we can gather some more supplies."

"Will anyone there help us?"

"I don't know." Snarly looked a little uncomfortable, a little embarrassed. "Um, I wasn't exactly honest before."

"What do you mean?" asked Tamryn.

Snarly looked at Normus. "I'm not the most popular guy in my village. In fact, I'm the least most popular."

"You mean you're not a big deal?" asked Normus.

"Well, I guess I'm a pretty big deal. Just, the opposite of how I said before. Everyone kind of hates me. A lot."

"Oh."

"Yeah. So, when we get there, let's just take things slow."

Snarly, Normus, and Tamryn arrived at the edge of the village just as the sun was setting over the horizon. They kept themselves hidden, until they could be sure the coast was clear. There wasn't a lot of activity, but a few folks were out, walking and talking. And a group of kids were in the middle of the road, playing a game of snackball.

Snackball was a truly disgusting game. It was invented during a time of war, when people were literally starving, and, for some bizarre reason, people just kept playing it. The ball was made from whatever discarded foods each kid could bring, whether they were from their house or from some random pile of trash on the ground. They would take these leftovers and mash them together, forming a ball that had to measure at least a foot across.

The rules of snackball were simple: Whoever had control of the ball would throw it high into the air, and then the rest of the players would try to be the next one to catch it. So, after this ball rolled around on the ground and was handled by a bunch of dirty kids, if you were lucky enough to catch it, you would get to take a big bite out of it. That may sound like the last thing you'd want to do, but every time you took a bite, you got a point. And whoever was able to catch it at the very end, putting that last bite-sized piece into their mouth, got an extra five points.

The snackball was only about halfway eaten, so it was going to be a while.

"This is your village?" asked Normus. "It's so big."

"It's actually the smallest one in the whole countryside," said Snarly. "But whatever…"

Tamryn stepped up between them. "So, what's the plan?

"We should wait here, wait for everyone to get off the streets, go to bed. We don't want anyone to see us."

"Why not?" asked Normus.

Snarly turned to face him. "You still don't get it, do you? These people are going to be terrified of you."

"Why?"

"Where have you been? We've already talked about this. At length! They're gonna take one look at you and assume you're the murderous Beast."

"But I'm not the Beast."

Snarly slapped his forehead. "Yes, but they don't know that. They're gonna judge you by your appearance, and they're gonna freak out."

"Well, that's not right. Maybe if they got to know me a little first."

Snarly shrugged. "You can try it. Go up and talk to them, see what happens."

"Really? Okay." Normus started to get up.

"Yeah, sure, why not. They'll probably kill you before you can even finish a sentence, but, hey, it's worth a shot."

Normus hesitated, then slowly sat back down. "Maybe I'll wait."

"Good idea," Snarly said. "You might as well get comfortable. We're going to be here for a while."

Tamryn squinted her eyes. "Are those kids *eating* that ball?"

Several hours later, after the village had quieted down and most of the lights in the cottages were out, Snarly elbowed

Normus, who was asleep. He got startled and rolled over on top of Tamryn, who let out a muffled scream.

"Ow!" squealed Normus as he jumped up. "You bit me!"

"I was suffocating on your fur!" said Tamryn. "I thought I was gonna die!"

"Will you two keep it down?" Snarly said in a loud whisper. "Be quiet and follow me."

(Remember when the final knight returned (sort of), and the mayor said they should build a wall around the village to protect themselves from the Beast? Well, it was very easy to get past that wall...because it wasn't there. Yeah, all that stuff they talked about—building a wall, making weapons— none of that happened. Snarly and the gang just had to step around a few bricks and they were in.)

Snarly led them through the dark alleyways that ran behind his home. The trek there was somewhat uneventful— a dog barked at them (and Normus barked back), they stepped on some dried twigs that made a lot of snapping sounds, and Tamryn sneezed quite loudly—and they felt very pleased with themselves for being so quiet and sneaky as they stepped up to the back door.

Snarly made a face. "That's weird," he whispered. "The door's unlocked." He opened it and they stepped inside... and heard voices! Laughter and talking! From the living room!

They froze.

Snarly looked around the kitchen and knew immediately what was wrong. They were in the wrong house! He caught Normus's and Tamryn's attention and motioned for them to tiptoe back toward the door.

The two nodded, but before they could move, an old man with very thick eyeglasses shuffled into the room. The three stood as still as statues, not even blinking. They followed the old man with their eyes as he went to the counter, picked up a spoon, and then went back to the other room, never even noticing the three "intruders" in his kitchen.

Snarly, Normus, and Tamryn hurried to the door (this time knocking over some pots and pans and making a *lot* of noise). Once outside, they ran as fast as they could around the corner.

"Who was that?" asked Normus.

"Those were the Flugeltonsons."

"What were they doing in your house?" asked Tamryn.

"That wasn't my house," Snarly said, still out of breath.

"What?"

"I had the wrong house."

"You don't even know your own house?"

"They all look the same from behind!" He almost said, *At least I have a house!*, but thought that was a bit too harsh. Instead, he pointed and said, "Mine's that way, two doors down."

"You sure about that?" asked Tamryn.

"Ha, ha. Just keep moving."

Moments later, they arrived at Snarly's house (and yes, it was the right house this time), but everything was gone! All of his furniture, all his appliances, his books, his food. Even his collection of antique whistles, gone! All gone!

"Where's all your stuff?" asked Tamryn.

Snarly's mouth hung open. "They took it. The vulchars took everything."

"Who did?" asked Normus.

"The villagers, my neighbors. They cleaned me out. Probably came in here as soon as I crossed over into the woods, those greedy, selfish, little…thieves!"

"Wow. That stinks," said Tamryn.

"I know, right?" said Snarly. "I can't believe them."

"No. I mean, *that* stinks." Tamryn pointed to a pile of rotten cabbage that had been thrown in a corner.

"Now why would they just leave that on the floor like that?" Snarly said, very annoyed. "That's some good snack-ball material right there."

After they cleaned up the moldy scraps of food left by the pillagers, they all settled down on the floor to get some sleep. The only problem with that was that they *couldn't* sleep.

After about a half an hour of just lying there with her eyes open, Tamryn said, "Snarly? You awake?"

He was, but he pretended not to be. He wasn't in the mood to talk. *Stupid, dumb neighbors…*

Tamryn rolled over. "Normus?"

Normus turned his head to look at her. "Yes, Tamryn?"

"Are you awake?" she asked.

"Yes. Unless this is a dream."

Tamryn smiled. "It's not a dream."

"Okay. Good."

"Are you scared, Normus?"

"A little. Yes."

Knowing that such a big guy could also get scared made Tamryn feel just a little bit better. "So, are you an orphan, too?" she asked.

"I'm not sure."

"Where are your parents?"

"I don't think I have parents."

"Well, you have to have parents," said Tamryn. "How else could you have been born?"

"I don't know."

"You don't remember them at all? Not even a little?"

"Nope."

"Well, I remember my parents."

"What happened to them?"

Tamryn hesitated, then said, "We were in an accident. There was a rockslide. We were traveling, and all these boulders fell from a cliff and crashed into our carriage. I almost didn't make it out, but Mr. Dacab—Macaberus Darc was there to rescue me."

"That was lucky."

Tamryn looked at him. "Was it?"

"What do you mean? Of course it was. If he hadn't been there, you might have died, too."

She got up on one elbow. "Do you think it's possible that Macaberus Darc caused the accident? That he killed my parents, just so he could take me as his little slave?"

Normus and Tamryn jumped as Snarly spoke up. "Of course it's possible. In fact, it's more than possible, it's probable. Macaberus Darc is an evil, evil man who will do anything to acquire that which he desires. In his weakened state,

163

he needed you to do the little things he couldn't do, like deliver bread bombs."

"But why me?" she asked, her voice cracking.

"Oh, I'm sure he didn't want you specifically," Snarly said through a yawn. "You were just in the wrong place at the wrong time."

There was a moment of silence. Then Tamryn sighed and said, "Then it *was* my fault."

"What was?" asked Snarly.

"My parents' death."

"How in the world was that your fault?"

"We were moving to a different village—my father had found a better job—but I didn't want to move, I wanted to stay with my friends. So I hid in an old treehouse. Not mine, but one that we had found. When my parents finally found me, I just cried and cried and refused to go with them. They practically had to drag me away."

After a while, Snarly grumbled. "And how does that make it your fault, child?"

"Because, if I hadn't acted like such a baby, we would have left on time. We wouldn't have been in the wrong place at the wrong time."

"You don't know what you're talking about," Snarly said. "There's no way you could know that for sure. You have no idea how long Darc was waiting there for someone to come by."

"Yeah," said Normus.

"See? Even he gets it. Now let's get some sleep. No more negative thoughts, okay? You'll feel better in the morning." (Whoa. Did Snarly just say not to have negative thoughts?)

164

"Okay," said Tamryn, and she tried to go to sleep, really she did, but every time she closed her eyes she saw her parents being crushed under the weight of all those boulders. And Macaberus Darc, disguised as an old man, laughing at her from the shadows.

Snarly could hear her softly crying, but he didn't think it wise to try to console her. *Just let her cry herself to sleep,* he thought. *She's gonna need it.* He knew that tomorrow was going to bring with it a whole new set of challenges. And the first of those challenges belonged to him and him alone...

Convincing the Villagers
(CHAPTER 21)

WHEN SNARLY AWOKE THE NEXT MORNING, HE THOUGHT it was just any other, normal morning. Until he realized he was lying on the floor. And every single one of his possessions had been stolen. Then he saw the little girl and the huge, lumbering monster lying on the floor and it all came back to him.

Oh, yeah, he thought, *my life is in complete turmoil. How could I have forgotten?*

He sat up and rubbed his eyes. He hadn't meant for them to sleep so late. He knew they should get going before someone saw them, and the longer they waited, more people would be out and about.

"Normus. Tamryn. We need to get going." He waited, but neither one stirred.

He tapped Tamryn on the shoulder. "Tamryn. Time to wake up."

Still nothing, so he slapped both of her shoulders at the same time. "Tamryn!" She jerked awake, frightened. "Hey, look who's up."

Tamryn rubbed her arms. "Did you hit me?" she asked.

Snarly shook his head innocently. "No. Why?"

"Must have been a dream."

"Weird. Well, we should really get moving. I know of one person who might actually listen to our plea without jumping to any hasty reactions."

"Who?"

"Jobos. He's never done anything hasty in his life. He's sort of the village idiot. At least, that's how I like to refer to him. If we can make it to him first, then perhaps he can talk to the mayor, and introduce our cause before they see *him*." He nodded his head toward Normus, who was still sleeping, his back leg twitching.

"Aw," Tamryn said. "He's dreaming. How cute."

"Yeah. It's adorable." Snarly slapped Normus on the leg. "Normus, time to wake up."

Nothing. *Oh, come on!*

"Normus!" He grabbed hold of both shoulders and began to rock him from side to side. "Normus! Normus, Normus, Normus! Wake up!" Snarly stopped, out of breath. It was really hard moving such a big creature like that. "This is hopeless! There's no waking him."

Just then, Tamryn jumped back with a squeak.

"What?" asked Snarly. "What's wrong?"

She relaxed. "I just saw a spider, that's all."

At the word *spider*, Normus was up and alert. "Spider? Where?" He ran and stood in a corner, looking all over the room with wide eyes.

"Seriously? You wake up to that?"

"You're afraid of spiders?" asked Tamryn with a smile.

"Yes," said Normus. He didn't even like the word *spi*— well, you know. "Was it a big one or a small one?"

"Oh, brother," said Snarly. "Look at you. Someone as big as you, crying over a spider."

"I don't like them. They're creepy. And now I'm all itchy, like they're crawling around in my fur."

"What a big baby," Snarly laughed.

"Leave him alone, Snarly. I don't like spiders, either."

Snarly shook his head. "We need to go. Jobos lives only a few houses down. Stay close to me, stay in the shadows, and keep quiet."

"Question."

"Yes, Normus?"

"Can we eat breakfast first?"

Snarly just looked at him. "Let's go."

Normus slumped his shoulders. "I'm hungry."

"Maybe this Jobos guy will have some food," Tamryn said.

"I hope so."

"Quiet." Snarly opened the back door, letting in the sunlight. He peeked around, saw no one, and then stepped out into the alleyway. "All right, quickly now."

They all stepped outside, and Tamryn quietly shut the door behind her.

"It's around this way," Snarly said, waving.

As they turned the corner and were about to cross the road, they stopped. Two women were talking to each other, their baby carriages next to them. Seeing that they weren't noticed, Snarly motioned for them to continue.

They tiptoed down the side of a house, and just as they were almost to the end and out of sight, Normus's stomach growled. The mothers and their babies turned, saw them, and started screaming at the top of their lungs.

Snarly held his hands up. "No, no, no." He tried to calm them, but with each movement the women and babies only screamed louder. It wasn't long before a crowd started to gather to see what was happening.

"What is *that*?" Some of them said, while pointing at Normus.

Finally, someone shouted, "It's the Beast!"

This was exactly what Snarly had been afraid of. "No, it's not," he said.

"And Snarly brought it here! Right into the midst of us!"

"No," he said. "It's not what you think."

"Who is that girl with them?" a woman asked.

"She's no one!" Snarly shouted, pointing a finger. "You leave her alone!"

"'Tain't no girl," another man said. "'Tis a witch! Here to help the Beast destroy us!"

"String 'em up!"

Great, Snarly thought. *Again with the hanging!*

"Hang them all!"

"Cleanse our village of these monsters!"

"No, you don't understand," said Tamryn.

"Quiet, witch!"

169

"I'm not a witch!"

"That's exactly what a witch would say!" one man said.

"That's what *I'd* say if *I* was a witch," confirmed the man's friend. The man looked over at him and the friend got real nervous. He held his hands up. "Not that I am a witch! 'Cause I ain't! I'm just saying."

"Everyone needs to just calm down," Snarly said.

"Quiet, you! You brought them here!"

"But he's not the Beast!" Snarly pleaded.

A little girl with a pale blue ribbon in her hair (you know the one) stepped up to the front of the mob, right in front of Normus.

"Jasmine! No!" Her mother tried to reach out for, but some men pulled her back.

"Are you crazy, lady? That's the Beast."

"That's my daughter!"

The crowd fell silent as the girl stepped up to Normus.

She held out a ball of yarn. Once she had his attention, she threw it high into the air.

Normus fell to the ground as he caught the yarn and began to play with it. He kicked at it with his back paws, bit into it. He was even purring.

One person smiled and said, "Would you look at that. It looks like an overgrown kitten."

"You see?" Snarly said. "The Beast wouldn't behave like that."

Another man was smiling. "Maybe he's right. Cute little guy, ain't he?"

"Well, why have you come back then?" a woman yelled. "Did you destroy the real Beast?"

"No," Snarly said, and a murmur rose from the crowd. "But I found him, the real Beast. *We* found him."

"'*Him*?'" someone asked.

"The Beast is a *he*?" someone else asked. "Surely not."

"It's some kind of animal, isn't it?"

"That's what I've always heard."

"The Beast is Macaberus Darc," Snarly interrupted. "The evil sorcerer."

"You lie!"

"Macaberus Darc was killed!"

"Or, at the very least, banished from this world!"

Tamryn weighed in. "It's true. It's all true. He was my guardian, disguised as an elderly man."

"He's growing in strength," Snarly said. "If we don't stop him now, it may be too late."

The crowd grew very restless at this news and talked amongst themselves at great length.

"What is to be done about this?" someone asked.

Snarly stood before his neighbors, people he had known his entire life, as a new man. He was now full of compassion, confidence, and purpose. He held his arms up and the crowd quieted. He said, "Tomorrow we go and destroy the Beast. We destroy Macaberus Darc, once and for all. We put an end to his reign of terror before he fully regains his strength. For at that point, all will be lost."

A woman in the crowd snorted. "And just how are we going to do that?"

He looked the crowd over carefully, then looked at his new friends, Normus and Tamryn.

"Together," he said.

Snarly took a deep breath. It looked like he had their attention. Now he would have to spend the rest of the day convincing them it was possible. They would have to come up with a plan. Where the knights failed them, Snarly would have to step up and—it was hard to even imagine—be the hero. There was a lot to be done, for tomorrow would be...

THE FINAL SHOWDOWN!
THE FINAL FIGHT!
THE BATTLE TO END ALL BATTLES!

THE DAY THEY TAKE DOWN THE BIG, MEAN VILLAIN!

THE VILLAIN WHO'S BEEN CAUSING
SO MANY PEOPLE
SO MANY PROBLEMS
FOR SO MANY YEARS!

THE VILLAIN WHOSE TIME HAS COME!

THE VILLAIN WHO'S ABOUT TO
MEET HIS MATCH!

WHO'S ABOUT TO MEET THE ONE WHO—

Um…sorry. Got a little carried away there.

(PART FIVE)

WELL, THAT WAS REALLY SOMETHING, HUH? SNARLY stepping up and rising to the occasion.

I, uh, just…um… Wow, uh, this has never happened to me before. I'm sorry. I'm getting a little emotional over here.

I know this should be an exciting time for us. We're about to start the thrilling conclusion, after all. But all I can think about right now is how much I'm going to miss you.

Yes, I know we'll never *really* be apart. I'll be sitting over on your bookshelf—or wherever you keep your books—but it won't be the same, you know? And I'm not gonna go through that whole thing where I make you promise you'll read the book again, just one more time, 'cause we all know how that goes.

Wait a minute. I almost forgot. The sequel! We can get back together for the sequel! Oh, rapture!

Never mind. We're cool. Sorry for making things all weird there, I just got a little panicked. But I'm good now. What say we get back into this story and have us the time of our lives, eh?

Yeah? Awesome! Good timing, too, because this is the chapter where…

The Village Sets Out
(CHAPTER 22)

ALMOST THE ENTIRE VILLAGE SET OUT THAT MORNING TO
confront Macaberus Darc. Snarly had done a good job
building morale among his neighbors. The only ones who
stayed behind were those unable to fight—children and the
elderly—and those that were needed to care for them.

Everyone carried a makeshift weapon of some sort. What
they hoped to accomplish going up against the evilest, vilest
sorcerer that ever lived with only pitchforks and rolling pins,
they didn't know. But they would try. They only knew that
they would not stand idly by and let their land become rav-
aged by that madman. Not again.

"I hope you know what you're doing," Tamryn said to
Snarly.

"I don't," he replied.

"I wish I could think of something else that might help us defeat Darc, but I had no idea who he was. He was just a mean old man who I had to obey because he gave me food and shelter. I wasn't looking for weaknesses."

"I understand," said Snarly. "Don't worry. One way or another, we'll get rid of him."

"Yeah," said Normus. "You'll never have to worry about him again, not as long as we're around. Right, Snarly?"

"That's right."

Tamryn didn't look so sure. "I hope so," she said quietly.

"There's nothing we 'best worst friends' can't do if we stick together," said Normus. He clapped his paws. "Hey, I just had an idea."

"What's that?" said Tamryn.

"It's like a thought," said Normus. "Like a thought that makes you think of something."

"I know what an idea is, Normus."

"Then why did you ask?"

Tamryn looked at Snarly, who just shrugged and said, "See what I've been dealing with?"

"What's your idea, big guy?"

"I was thinking, do you think the other villagers would want to join the Best Worst Friends Club? We'd have so many members then. We'd have to meet in a convention center or someplace!"

"The what?" asked Snarly.

"Oh, yeah," said Normus. "You weren't there for that. We formed a club."

Tamryn smiled. "I don't know how many folks would be interested in that."

"Well, I'll go ask around a bit, see if I can't generate some interest."

"You do that, pal." Snarly smiled and shook his head as he watched Normus walk away.

Shortly after, Mayor Mayer stepped between Snarly and Tamryn and started walking alongside them. "So, Snarly, my friend, you really think this foolproof plan of yours is going to work?"

"It's hardly foolproof, Mayor."

Mayer leaned in, said quieter, "It is gonna work, though, right? Please tell me it's gonna work."

"I can't make any promises. Tamryn will lead us to the shack where Darc's been living. I'm going to try to reason with him, give him one last chance to leave our land."

"Then what?" asked Mayer. "What if he doesn't leave? What if he just laughs in your face?"

Snarly shrugged. "I don't know. We'll make him leave."

"How?"

"Well, I haven't gotten that far."

"What?"

"Don't worry about it," Snarly said. "We'll just have to...improvise."

"Improvise? Now, Snarly, when I agreed to come along and put my neck on the line in order to help you rally the others, I thought you had a plan. That's how you made it seem, at least. You didn't say anything about improvising."

"As long as we stick together, everything will be fine. There are way more of us than him." Snarly nodded toward Tamryn, who looked pretty nervous. "Maybe we should change the subject, yeah?"

Mayor Mayer took the hint. "Yes. Yes, you're right. Just a case of the nerves. You know, Tamryn, this is a very brave thing you're doing, and we all greatly appreciate it."

"Thank you, sir."

"And don't you worry about a thing, we won't let anything happen to you."

Tamryn appreciated the sentiment, but she had her doubts as to whether or not anyone could stop Macaberus Darc. As she remembered how huge he had gotten when he attacked them earlier, she hoped they weren't too late and that he was still weak enough to stop.

It was a long walk after that. People kept coming to Snarly, Tamryn, and Normus, wanting words of encouragement, wanting to know the big plan. Snarly just kept talking, kept leading them on, kept trying to keep their spirits up.

Honestly, he didn't know what was going to happen. He didn't know how strong Darc was. All he knew for certain was that something had to be done. This was for everyone— all the people of the land, his village, himself, Tamryn, even Brutus. Someone had to stand up for them.

He had changed direction at one point in the journey. He didn't want to, but he knew they were going to need all the help they could get.

Snarly stopped and held up a hand, signaling the rest of the group. "We're here," he said. "Everyone just stay here. I'll go up alone."

Tamryn and Normus stepped up to him. "What's this?" Tamryn asked.

"It's a bridge, silly," said Normus. "Even I know that."

"I know it's a bridge, Normus. Who are we supposed to be meeting here?"

"Someone who may be able to help us," Snarly said. "His name is Boggwyn."

"Who?" asked Tamryn.

"Boggwyn. He's the troll that guards this bridge."

"They do that?"

"That's what I said!"

"I thought trolls were mean."

"Not this one," Snarly assured her. "He seems like kind of a scaredy-cat, but he's a troll, which means he's strong. And we can use a little more strength."

"Well," said Tamryn, "me and Normus will come with you, just in case."

"No, that's okay," said Snarly. "I can handle it."

"Maybe, but we're still coming."

Normus put a paw on his shoulder. "The BWFC always sticks together."

Snarly shook his head. "Whatever. Let's just get this over with."

They stepped up to the bridge, and Snarly called out, "Boggwyn!" There was no response. "Boggwyn?" Nothing. "Hmm. I hope he's not gone for too long."

"Maybe we have to actually try to cross the bridge," Tamryn said. "Like in the stories."

"I already called for him," Snarly said. "I doubt he'd be so—" But then he thought about it. "Yeah, I could see that."

So they started to cross the bridge, and as soon as they did they heard a voice: "Who goes there?"

"Boggwyn, come on!" Snarly yelled. "I know you heard us talking."

Boggwyn came out from under the bridge. "Yeah, I did. Sorry. I just have a process, you know? Gotta follow the script." Once he was standing in front of them he held his arms out. "Snarly! My old friend! How have you been? Did you slay the Beast? Did you use the rock?"

"No," said Snarly. "I didn't slay the Beast. Not yet, anyway. That's why we're here." He motioned behind him, where the crowd of villagers stood.

Boggwyn waved. "Hello."

The villagers waved back. They had never seen such a short troll before.

"We're on our way to slay the Beast now. It's actually Macaberus Darc. Have you heard of him?"

"You mean the evil sorcerer that kills and steals and turns bad little trolls into inside-out frogs?"

"I take it you were told stories as a kid?"

"Oh, yeah. Every time I would do something wrong, my mother would tell me all about Macaberus Darc, and how, if I didn't stop wetting the bed or hitting my sister or eating the flowers out of the neighbor's garden, he would sneak in through my window at night and blow his magic poison dust on me."

"That's horrible!" said Tamryn.

"I know. The worst part was that I didn't even have a window in my room. So how could I lock it or anything to keep him from coming in?"

"No, I mean it's horrible that your mother would tell you such stories."

"What do you mean? She was just warning me."

"Anyway!" Snarly interrupted. "We're looking for help, Boggwyn. Can we count on you to fight beside us?"

"Say what?"

"Will you fight with us?"

Boggwyn started fidgeting with his hands. "Fight? Uh, no. Sorry. But I can give you some more rocks." He started to go get some. "You can take all the rocks you need."

"Rocks won't help!"

"But what if some punk kids come along with some spray paint? Who will stop them if I'm not here?"

"Have there *ever* been kids with spray paint?"

"Well, no. But there's a first time for everything."

Tamryn stepped up. "Please, Boggwyn. We need your help. This affects you, too. If Macaberus Darc regains his strength, he'll destroy everything, including this bridge, your home. Don't you see? There won't be a bridge to protect."

Boggwyn dropped his head. "But, I'm no match for a sorcerer."

Normus knelt beside him and placed a paw on his back. "I'm scared, too. But together, I believe we can defeat him."

Boggwyn looked up at Normus, then at Tamryn and Snarly. He smiled, unsure.

Quietly, he said, "Let me just grab a couple rocks."

"We don't need any—" Snarly started, but then thought, *Whatever makes you feel better.*

The group had crossed over into the Black Forest and were making excellent time. Festus caught up to Snarly and said, "This is a good thing you're doing, Son. I didn't know you had it in you."

"Thank you, but I don't feel like we've got much of a choice. We either stop him or we die. Or we become his slaves. Or worse."

"Yeah, well, I just never saw you as the rally-the-troops kind of guy. You've grown a lot in the past few days."

"Thanks."

"Well, I always knew he would grow up to be someone great," Brunhildia said. "And now look at him, saving the world." She threw her arms around his neck and started crying again. "I'm so proud of you!"

Snarly freed himself and rubbed his neck. "Come on, Mother, everyone's watching you. Calm down."

"Sorry. Sorry, everyone!"

"We're here," Snarly said and sighed. "Let's see if I can talk one more guy into helping us."

"Another friend?"

"Sort of. He's a centaur."

Festus looked impressed. "A centaur? Yes, that would certainly help. Centaurs make great warriors."

"This centaur is a little, well, you'll see. His name is Handell."

Snarly figured if he was going to get the help of the townspeople and Boggwyn the troll, he...

Might as Well Round Everyone Else Up, Right?

(CHAPTER 23)

"HANDELL, HUH?"

"That's right!" Handell galloped into the clearing, standing between the intruders and his Fountain of Jubilation. "'Handell!'" he declared. "Keeper of the—Ah! What is that? Is that a troll?"

Snarly stepped forward. "Yes, Boggwyn is a troll, but he means no harm."

Handell raised an eyebrow. "What's wrong with it?"

"What do you mean?" said Snarly.

"Hey. Nothing's wrong with me!" said Boggwyn.

"He's tiny," chuckled Handell.

"Well, he's hardly tiny."

"I am a dwarf troll!"

Handell recognized Snarly for the first time and smiled. "Hey! I know you. Come back to try again the sadness-healing waters of the—" Handell clomped his hooves into the grass and then proudly puffed up his chest. "—Fountain of Jubilation!"

"No," Snarly said, matter-of-factly. "We've come to ask for your help."

"Help getting those frowns turned upside down?"

"No, we—"

"Help getting that pep back in your step?"

"What? No—"

"Help calling forth your inner child—"

"No!" Snarly screamed, causing Handell to take a step back. "We are looking for those brave enough to help us slay the true Beast, Macaberus Darc, evil sorcerer and all-around dirty scumbag."

Handell laughed. "Macaberus Darc?" He laughed some more. "You are a strange one, Snaggly Littlebutt."

"It's Snarly Smallbottom."

"Whatever you call yourself! Macaberus Darc is dead, has been for years."

"He's not. Me, that girl, and this furry thing saw him ourselves. We barely got away with our lives."

Handell cocked his head and then circled Normus. "And what, exactly, is this 'furry thing'?"

"This is Normus," said Snarly. "Say hello, Normus."

"Hello, horsie-man."

Handell raised an eyebrow, then laughed heartily. "You keep very strange friends, Snarly. I am happy to consider myself one of them. Now, what was it you were saying?"

"We need help," Snarly pleaded. "We are on our way to confront Macaberus Darc and force him from this land. But we must hurry. He's building his magical strength as we speak."

"Then you've got a death wish, my little friend." He faced the crowd. "All of you people do!"

"We have to stop him."

" 'We?' I'm sorry, but my place is here."

"There won't *be* a here if Macaberus Darc gets his way!" Snarly shouted. "Your fountain will be his! He'll turn these waters into poison, or something!"

"I'm sorry. I cannot help you."

Festus stepped forward. "Sir. I am just a simple farmer. I'm old, and I'm weak. But Snarly is my son, and I believe him. I also believe *in* him. If he says we're all in danger, then we're *all* in danger. And it's going to take all of us to stop this madman."

Handell thought about it, looked the crowd over again. "You folks are out of your minds."

"Maybe," said Festus. "But I know of your people, the centaurs. Centaurs are great warriors, brave and true."

"Well..." Handell said with a smile.

"No, no, it's a fact. At every great battle, at every great victory, at every great achievement and advancement this world has ever known, a centaur was present."

"We are magnificent creatures."

"That you are, mighty Handell," continued Festus. "Now, I ask you, shouldn't a centaur be there when Macaberus Darc is finally put down? Wouldn't *you* like to be there? Wouldn't you like to be that centaur, standing there, gallantly, when the world sings of those heroes who felled that great and terrible villain?"

Handell pondered this, pictured it in his mind, then said loudly, so all could hear, "For those of you seeking bravery, I can offer you a drink from the Fountain of Jubilation. It will grant you unconditional happiness, high spirits, and contentment. Perhaps that will give you an edge in battle." He took a deep breath. "And for those of you seeking protection and aid, I offer you myself. I will be *that* centaur. I will fight alongside you, my friends and neighbors."

The group cheered as Handell bowed, and then they began lining up for a drink from the fountain.

"No need to applaud me. I am only Handell, son of Fawndell, grandson of Tyrell, cousin to Syndell…"

Festus looked to Snarly and smiled. "I also know that centaurs have huge egos."

Snarly clapped him on the back. "Good job, Father."

They journeyed for hours—through the Black Forest, into the Pretty Forest—until it was time to make camp. They would need their rest if they were to succeed against Darc.

"It's getting late," Snarly said. "We should find a place to make camp. We can sleep in shifts, some staying up to keep watch, just in case. For all we know, Darc has a crystal ball or magic mirror or something and is watching us."

Handell trotted up. "You know, Snarly, I believe there's a B and B not too far—"

"No!" Snarly yelled. His lip started twitching, and he pulled it down to keep it from turning into a smile. "No B and B! We sleep outside!"

"Okay." Handell watched as Snarly walked away. He turned to Normus. "What was that all about?"

That night, Snarly dreamed that he'd gotten lost in a thick fog, separated from the group. He wandered through the forest, his movements sluggish, the sounds around him distorted and vague.

After a while, he heard the stomping of heavy footfalls in the distance, and he knew it was Goggy Blass. He tried to go the opposite direction, but he couldn't seem to avoid the advancing rumble of those giant feet.

Then Goggy Blass appeared, but only as a silhouette, a shadow, a dark, fluttering ghost in the fog. He didn't attack Snarly, he just stood back, menacingly. A foreshadowing of things to come?

As Snarly stared at the form of the deadly ogre, a maniacal laughter arose. It grew in intensity, seemingly in rhythm with the parting of the fog, which seemed to dance around him and then float away until finally revealing the vile Macaberus Darc.

Darc was huge, just like before, and behind him stood a massive castle. It looked like a haunted mansion, old and creepy, windowless and ancient. Lightning flashed from a cloudless sky, basking the sorcerer in a sort of pale, sickly, purple light.

Darc glanced to the side and stopped laughing when he saw Normus. He bared his teeth and hissed at the unwelcome animal, then shot a beam of dark purple light from his staff.

Snarly ducked down, but the bolt never came. He looked up to see Normus giggling and holding his belly.

"That tickles," he said.

Darc howled, angry at the foolish creature for daring to get in his way. He waved his staff in the air again, tried to shoot another bolt at Snarly, but it was also blocked.

In the fog of the dream, Snarly couldn't really tell what was happening. Was Normus eating the bolts of light? It looked more like he was jumping in front of Snarly and absorbing the attack somehow.

"What do you think of that, Snarly?" asked Normus as he hopped around like an idiot.

"Quiet, you idiot!" whispered Snarly. "Get down, before Darc hits us!"

"Oh, he can't hurt me! Ha, ha!"

"Get down!"

"He can't hurt me! Can he, Snarly?" Normus was laughing and jumping, blocking the repeated shots from Darc's staff. "Nothing he does can affect me! See how he can't hurt me, Snarly? See, Snarly? Snarly?"

"Snarly!!"

"Ah!" Snarly jumped up, holding his chest. "What?"

Normus was crouched down next to him. "You wouldn't wake up," he said. "I thought you were in a death sleep."

"What? What's a death sleep?"

"I don't know. That's why I was so freaked out."

Snarly scowled at him. "Get off of me!"

"Come on!" Normus called as he skipped away. "There's breakfast!"

But Snarly couldn't stop thinking about the dream. Did it mean something? Was it a premonition? Or was it just a nightmare brought on by stress?

"Come on!" Normus yelled as he ran toward the food.

Snarly wasn't hungry, but he knew he should eat something. There was still one more stop they had to make before confronting Darc.

Snarly stood before the group, his hands high in the air so they could see him. "All right, everyone. One last stop."

Tamryn recognized where they were. She said, "You don't mean—"

"I do." Snarly said with a smile. "We can easily get some help here. All we have to is walk up and ask for it."

"What is this place, Son?" asked Festus.

"You'll see."

"Hey," Handell whinnied. "I know this place. I play volleyball with these guys sometimes."

"Doesn't surprise me a bit," Snarly said. "Everyone stay here till I signal for you. Normus, Tamryn, and Handell, you're with me." And then he walked onto the grounds of the knights' little retirement village.

"Hey, guys! Guess who's back!" shouted Dollin. He was playing horseshoes with Fillop. "See, Fillop, I told you. Snarly! Remember him?"

"Why, yes I—" he began, but then quickly threw down the horseshoes when he saw Handell.

Dollin tossed his horseshoes aside, too. "Handell!" he said. "Come for a game of volleyball?"

"No, Dollin, we are here on more pressing matters." He looked down. "Hey! Those are my shoes! I've been looking all over for those!"

"Oh, hey. How did those get here?"

"Pressing matters, you say?" Maxus came walking over with several of the other knights.

"That's right," Snarly said.

"He's a persistent little thing, isn't he?" laughed Xavier.

"I thought I told you," said Maxus, "we aren't doing the whole 'helping' thing anymore."

"Oh, I know," said Snarly. "But maybe you'd like to explain that to my friends." He whistled for everyone to come out. "I think you remember them, don't you?" Snarly smiled. "I know they remember you."

Instantly, all the knights stepped back. Maxus had his hands in the air. "Whoa! Whoa, whoa, whoa!"

"I'm not even moving," Handell said.

Mayor Mayer stepped to the front of the crowd. He couldn't believe what he was seeing. "What is this?"

"Now, now, Mayor," said Maxus, "This isn't what it looks like."

191

"No," said Snarly. "There's a perfectly reasonable explanation for this."

"Oh?" said the mayor.

"Yeah. Right, Maxus?"

Maxus opened his mouth, but no words would come out.

"They've been here this whole time?" someone shouted.

"While we've been living in fear?" a woman yelled.

"We wrote songs about these jerks!"

"This is all just a big misunderstanding," said Maxus.

"Yeah," said Clotus. "We didn't even think there *was* a Beast."

Maxus quickly added, "But now that we know it was Macaberus Darc the whole time—"

"Hang 'em all!" someone screamed.

That's when Snarly stepped forward. "Calm down! Guys, what is it with you and the hanging? You've never hanged anyone, so why does someone always have to throw that out there?"

"Let them be the first to hang then!"

"They deserve it!"

"Maybe they do," Snarly said, "but we need them right now."

"That's right," said Xavier. "You—you need us."

"And I'm sure they would all love to help us in defeating Macaberus Darc," Snarly said. "Right, guys?"

The knights looked at each other, then looked at the angry mob.

"Of course," said Maxus. "Of course we would. We'll just, uh, get our things."

"But what about our new vow?" asked Clotus.

Maxus slapped him. "Oh, shut up!"

The rest of the trip was made in relative silence. They knew they were getting close—they could feel it—and it was putting everyone in a very solemn mood.

The knights got a lot of dirty looks from the villagers, so they pretty much just kept their heads down. They would certainly have to prove their worth in order to be forgiven.

When they finally reached the spot where Tamryn lived, everyone was stunned.

"I think his power is back," whispered Normus.

Snarly nodded. "Yeah."

Where there should have been an old, dilapidated shack, there now stood...

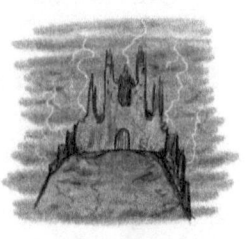

Darc's Castle

(CHAPTER 24)

SNARLY WAS AMAZED. IT WAS THE SAME CASTLE FROM HIS dream, the same dark, gloomy fortress. But how was that possible? *What is happening to me,* he thought.

The castle was bigger than anything he had ever seen before, and it was heavily fortified. The entire thing was perfectly impenetrable.

There was only one way in, and that was over the moat. The drawbridge had been descended. Just for them. And there it waited, daring anyone who may be foolish enough to cross it and step inside the dark castle.

But at least Darc didn't have an army.

Or did he? For all Snarly knew, he could have conjured one up. An army of zombies, an army of skeletons, of huge, hairy beasts, lizard men, whatever he wanted.

But Snarly didn't think so. No, this castle was meant to keep everyone out and to keep Darc safe until his magical powers were fully restored. He didn't need an army. He never did. All he ever needed was a little more time.

But Snarly wasn't going to give it to him.

He stepped forward, followed closely by Normus and Tamryn. And behind them stood the rest of his friends. He stopped at the edge of the drawbridge. Confident, he shouted, "Macaberus Darc! Come out now and surrender!"

Everyone waited. All was silent. They started to think that maybe he hadn't heard.

"Maybe he's not home?" Normus asked.

But then the ground began to shake, slightly at first. A faint laughter came from within the castle walls. It sounded far away, quiet, but it quickly grew, both in volume and intensity. Soon, the ground was shaking violently, and the entire sky was filled with the maniacal laughter of the insane Macaberus Darc. Everyone was frightened, not knowing what to do or where to hide.

Then, to make matters worse, thunder boomed and lightning flashed. The people were in awe, for there was not a cloud in the sky.

"Oh boy," Snarly said.

Tamryn tried to keep herself steady on the shaky ground, tried to yell over the thunder and lightning that was raging above them. "What do we do now?"

"I think it might be a good idea to run!" shouted Snarly.

"I think you're right!"

The trio ran back toward the group, covering their ears. Snarly assumed they would all be running away as well, but they were just standing there, looking up at the sky. "What are you doing?" he yelled at Handell. "We need to get out of here!"

But Handell could only point, his hand trembling.

When Snarly looked up, his heart sank. It was too late.

Arms outstretched, black robe flowing in the wind, Macaberus Darc slowly descended from the sky. His eyes, sunken in and dark, glowed a deep, dark purple. His fingernails were long and yellow.

The people were frozen, staring up in awe. Never had they seen such evil, and it was all encased in the body of one man.

When his feet finally touched the ground, Darc looked at Snarly and his friends. He smiled, hatred filling his eyes. "Oh, I'm gonna enjoy this," he said.

Snarly knew then, after looking into Darc's eyes, that there was no way they could hope to win...

The Final Fight

(CHAPTER 25)

"YOU'VE BEEN A VERY NAUGHTY GIRL, TAMRYN," DARC said. He looked at her as though she had betrayed him, when he was the one, after all, who had mistreated her and lied to her for so long. "I'm very disappointed in you."

"Leave her alone," Snarly said, stepping forward. "If you want to talk to someone, you talk to—"

"Silence!" Darc threw a hand out and Snarly flew back, as if slapped by an invisible force. He was knocked unconscious and landed a few feet away.

Tamryn and Normus tried to run to him—"Snarly!"— but they were whisked up into the air by unseen hands.

Macaberus held them there, thirty feet in the air, his staff glowing fiercely, his old face twisted in an unnatural, ruthless anger.

As he held Tamryn and Normus in the air with his staff, he turned to the crowd of villagers. "And what do we have here?"

The knights stepped forward. Maxus said, "Don't even think about it!"

"Oh, please," said Darc. "You had your chance to defeat me. Go back to your little clubhouse." And with a sweeping, circular motion of his hand, he transported the twelve knights right back to their home.

A collective gasp came from the crowd. They tried to step back, but Macaberus stopped them. He reached out—his hand looked like it was holding a cup—and kept them fastened to the ground. With a flick of his other wrist, he tossed Tamryn and Normus through the air. They landed in a group of bushes.

Macaberus was then free to hold the crowd of villagers with one hand and point the staff at them with the other. He slowly brought them closer, their feet dragging in the earth. When they were close enough that he could see into their eyes, he slowly closed his hand into a fist, squeezing them. They could feel the pressure becoming greater and greater. They all dropped their weapons, fearful.

"That's right," Darc said. "Give up. Surrender. It's hopeless. What are you against me?"

Then, charging full force, each one shouting a victory cry, Handell and Boggwyn, one on the left side of Darc, one on the right, leapt from the tree line, high into the air. Handell had his spear raised high, and Boggwyn's arm was reared back, ready to launch a heavy stone against the villain.

Macaberus smiled. He dropped the puny villagers, went down to one knee, and magically "grabbed" Handell and Boggwyn, and then used their own momentum to slam them into each other midair. The two heroes fell to the ground.

Macaberus swung his staff, round and round, over his head. Boggwyn and Handell spun in like fashion on the ground and then shot high into the air. The crowd of villagers watched as the two flew up and out of sight.

Snarly regained consciousness just in time to see the horrified faces of the villagers. He followed their eyes up into the air, where he saw Handell and Boggwyn, falling from a very high altitude.

"Should I catch them?" Darc asked. "Or should we watch them go *splat*?"

The crowd was too scared to say anything. At the last second, Darc stuck out his hand and caught the two of them. Boggwyn and Handell hung in the air a moment, until Darc tipped his hand over, then they fell the rest of the way.

As Darc laughed hysterically, Snarly saw Tamryn and Normus emerge from the bushes. They looked at each other and nodded, each knowing what to do.

Snarly went first. He deliberately walked into Darc's line of sight, trying to draw his attention. When Macaberus saw him, he threw a clenched hand in his direction, grabbing hold of Snarly.

As Normus walked toward the evil Macaberus Darc, he saw that Snarly was grabbing his chest, struggling to breathe. Without hesitation, he turned to Tamryn. "Get back. Behind the trees."

"But—"

"Now!" he roared. Yes, he scared her, and he didn't like to see her run away from him with tears in her eyes, but he had to make sure she was safe.

Nostrils flared, Normus marched up to Macaberus Darc and grabbed him from behind.

"Unhand me, you stupid beast!"

Normus turned Macaberus so that they were face to face. He roared, "I am not a Beast! I am E. Normus Furrybottom! And those are my friends!" He then snatched the staff from Darc's hand and threw Darc to the ground.

"No!" Darc screamed, fearful for the first time in a long time. "Give that back!"

"You're through," said Normus. And then, with one hand, he broke the staff in half.

With the crack of the wood came a blinding light. Everyone dropped to their knees and shielded their eyes. Normus and the sorcerer were thrown from each other in a massive explosion of energy. When those in the crowd opened their eyes again, Macaberus was gone, and Normus was twenty feet away, unconscious.

The people surrounded Normus, concerned, looking for any sign of life, as Snarly and Tamryn made their way through and knelt down on each side of him.

"He's breathing," Snarly said. "I think he'll be okay."

Boggwyn said, "What happened to Macaberus Darc?"

"Did anyone see anything?" asked Handell.

"I saw," said a man in the crowd. "He disappeared!"

"Disappeared?"

"He was defeated!" shouted a woman.

The crowd cheered, but Snarly cast a solemn look at Tamryn. "I don't think we've seen the last of Macaberus Darc."

"I think you're right," she said.

Snarly and Tamryn turned their attention to Normus. They did all they could to rouse him. They even pretended to see a family of giant spiders, but nothing worked.

"Oh, Normus," Tamryn said, "please be okay."

But Normus wasn't moving, and his breathing was shallow.

"Come on, Normus," Snarly said. "Get up, you big, ugly Beast."

"I'm not a Beast." It was barely above a whisper, but Normus said it.

Snarly smiled. "I knew that would get you."

Normus slowly opened his eyes. "What happened?"

"You did it."

"I did?"

"Yes," said Snarly. "I don't know how, but you defeated Macaberus Darc."

"Wow."

"You also called yourself Normus Furrybottom."

"I finally chose a last name. I named myself after you, Mr. Smallbottom."

Tamryn laughed. "Your last name is Smallbottom?"

"Yes. Ha, ha. Very funny."

"No, it's actually very fitting," she said, looking behind him. "I don't think I've ever seen one so small."

They laughed as the crowd cheered and helped them to their feet.

A few yards away, though, another was laughing, but for a completely different reason. It was a tiny insect, sitting on a blade of grass. It was rubbing its little legs together and cackling. It was so small that no one else could hear it.

It was Macaberus Darc! He had shape-shifted into an insect at the very last possible second.

He flew up into the air, triumphant, and circled the group. He looked down on the fools, laughing. He would be victorious, nothing could stop him, now that his power was fully restored.

They began to quiet down, one by one, as they each started to hear it. A tiny, high-pitched laugh that grew as Macaberus Darc grew.

Tamryn looked up to see a bug with the head of Darc flying toward Snarly. Darc was going to make one last attempt to slay him. She saw him lift his bug-like arms over his head, maniacally, ready to cast his most awful spell ever.

"Snarly!" she screamed.

Snarly and Normus turned, and to their amazement, flying right at them, was Macaberus Darc in the form of a bug.

And then—*PHTT!*

They looked very confused as they watched the freaky-looking Macaberus-bug fly in reverse. At least, that's what they both thought, until they saw the huge toad sitting in front of them.

"You!" Snarly said as he recognized the toad.

"Yes, me."

"Whoa," said Tamryn. "A talking toad."

"Actually…" said the toad as a thick cloud began to seep out of its mouth and nostrils. The cloud swirled around and around as the toad grew in size, until finally getting carried away by the wind.

Snarly's jaw dropped. "It's the Great Wizard," he said. "Oren Lightenshade!"

"That's right, young Snarly Smallbottom."

Tamryn snorted as she laughed. "Smallbottom. It's too much."

Snarly threw a glance at her. "Shut it." Then he turned back to the Great Wizard. "So, you were the toad I talked to as I entered the Black Forest?"

"Yes. I've been following you for quite some time, taking many forms, ever since you were first assigned to find and slay the Beast."

"You've been in my dreams," Snarly said, amazed. "You were the wolf, the deer? You've been guiding me."

"Yes."

"But why?"

"I've been waiting for someone brave enough to help me on my quest."

"You could have used anyone. Why me?"

"Many years ago, my powers were weakened to an extreme, and they've never fully recovered. My time on this earth is growing short, and I had to see Macaberus Darc defeated."

Lightenshade sat on a nearby boulder, then continued. "During our last battle, we both had the same idea, he and I: to change shapes into something smaller, something no one would notice. We were weak, so we used the last of our power to attack each other and then *pretended* to be defeated ourselves.

"We both assumed that the other had been destroyed, but something kept me from changing back to my normal self. I had a feeling that Macaberus may have had a similar idea. If he were weak, like me, he would have had to stay hidden until his magical strength was restored."

Lightenshade laughed quietly. "And I knew Macaberus well enough to know that he couldn't stay out of trouble, not for very long, anyway. He would surely try some type of scheme." Lightenshade held up a finger. "But, if he knew I was still alive, he would wait until his magic was fully restored, and then there would have been nothing I could have done. I needed him weak, so that I could take care of the problem, once and for all."

"Why not just tell me?" asked Snarly.

"I couldn't risk anything going wrong," said Lightenshade. "After the knights of Sandwich Town all ran away from their responsibilities, how could I be sure you wouldn't do the same? So, I led you to a creature that I thought would be a great help."

"What creature?"

Lightenshade smiled and pointed to Normus. "Him."

"Normus?!"

"Normus, as you call him, comes from a very old line of creatures that have a certain magical resistance. Normus is a boonbear—most likely the last of his kind—and very strong against magic. The evil side, Macaberus Darc and all his hoodlum friends, tried to kill them all."

"Why?"

"Because they are a great threat," said Lightenshade. "Other than a fellow wizard or witch, no one can stop

Macaberus and his villainous friends. I've stayed close to young Normus here for many years, trying to protect him from Macaberus Darc. But, alas, the time had come. When you were sent to slay the so-called Beast, I did my best to lead you to Normus."

"This is unbelievable," Snarly said. He looked up, disgusted. "And you just *ate* him?"

"Oh yes," the Great Wizard said as he patted his belly. "He's done for."

"So, what now?" asked Tamryn.

"Well, I suppose the three of you will be celebrated as heroes. Go home and enjoy your fame. As for me, I've been in hiding for so long, there are a few things I must take care of, one of which involves a very old friend." Lightenshade stood up, then smiled at Snarly. "I must say, Snarly, I'm very proud of you."

"Why?"

"You've come a long way from where you started. All you really needed to defeat Macaberus Darc was Normus, but I'm very impressed at how you've brought everyone together like this. You've gone above and beyond what I thought you were capable of."

Snarly blushed. "Aw, shucks."

"Until next time, my friends!" And with that, the Great Wizard, Oren Lightenshade, turned into an eagle and flew away.

Everyone just looked at each other, and then someone shouted, "Let's hear it for Snarly and company!" The three friends smiled at each other as a cheerful roar came up from the crowd.

And from that day forward, life was much better for the three heroes, though not perfect. Snarly was still grumpy, just not *as* grumpy. Normus was no longer looked at as a Beast, but as the magical hero that he was. And Tamryn had a family again and was beginning to find that there was a purpose to her life, not just to serve some old tyrant.

I would be more than happy to end this story with *And they lived happily ever after...,* but I'm afraid I can't honestly say that at this point. This story is far from over. If you thought this adventure was scary and dangerous, you have no idea.

But before you go, how about an...

Epilogue
ONE PLUS ONE PLUS ONE EQUALS THREE

(THERE. NOW YOU CAN TELL YOUR PARENTS THAT THIS book was not only exciting, entertaining, and worth every penny, but that it also helped you with your math.)

Snarly went into his small kitchen to make breakfast only to find that Normus and Tamryn were already eating. He squeezed past them, trying to get to the coffee.

The house was furnished again, by the way. Everyone brought back all the stuff they had taken, not that it was all in the same condition as when they took it—the jars of food were half-eaten, some of the furniture was scratched up— but at least his home was his home again.

The problem now, though, was that there wasn't enough room for everything, not with the addition of Tamryn and big ol' Normus.

They were also seeing a lot more of Brutus lately (he really enjoyed all the extra attention he was getting from Tamryn, and he loved cuddling up with Normus, who was like a giant, fuzzy cat bed).

"We need a bigger house," Snarly grumbled.

"Agreed," said Tamryn. "With a second bathroom."

"And more food." That was Normus, obviously.

"And who's going to pay for this extra bathroom and food?"

"You are," said Tamryn.

"I doubt that very much, thank you," Snarly said as he took a bite out of an apple. "We should all pitch in."

Tamryn said, "We're just kidding, Snarly."

"We are?" asked Normus.

"Of course we'll pitch in."

"We will?"

"Yes, Normus. It's the least we can do. We're a family now. We're in this together." She tore off a piece of bread and thought for a moment. "If only I had a job…"

"Yeah, that would help," Snarly said.

And then, right on cue, the shouting started again. Only this time they weren't running past Snarly's house, they were running into it.

"Snarly! He's coming!"

"Slow down, Jobos. Who's coming?"

"Goggy Blass! Goggy Blass is declaring war on all the villages. Says they're his!"

Tamryn jumped out of her seat. "Let's go!"

"What?" Snarly motioned for her to sit back down. "You're crazy! We're not going anywhere. That guy's insane."

Tamryn asked Jobos, "Is there a reward?"

"I would imagine so. Most likely a handsome one."

"See, Snarly? We can do this. We can defeat Goggy Blass, claim the reward, and get a bigger house!"

"You don't really know anything about Goggy Blass, do you?"

"No," said Tamryn, "but I know we can stop him."

"And how do you know that?" Snarly asked.

She pointed at Normus. "Because we have him."

Normus looked up from the table, jam dripping from the fur on his chin. "Me?"

AND THAT'S IT. GREAT BOOK, HUH?

Well, I'll see you next time! Thanks for reading!

What?

Oh, that's right! I did say something about a sequel earlier. I bet you want an exclusive sneak peek, don't ya?

Well, all right. How can I say no to you? Go ahead and turn the page for...

A SNEAK PEEK AT

NORMUS

SNARLY and the ~~BEAST~~ and TAMRYN

An Ocean Adventure

(There is no foreseeable release date
and
all material in this preview may be subject to change.
(Just so you know.))

CHAPTER ONE

Snarly woke up to the most awful smell. *What in the world is that?* he thought.

Well, there ya go! Stay tuned for more!
What? You don't want me to give away *too* much, do you?

ART GALLERY
CHARACTER SKETCHES

Snarly

Normus

Tamryn

Boggwyn

the

Troll

Handell

Jasmine

Jobos

Ma + Pa Vittle's
Bed
+
Breakfast

Macaberus
Darc

Oren
Lightenshade